THE SURROGATE

THE SURROGATE

DIOGENES KAUFMAN

trash panda
press

Published by Trash Panda Press

ISBN 978-1-7362544-9-3

Typesetting services by BOOKOW.COM

To people who live in little towns and refuse to be quiet.

PREFACE

The following is a work of fiction. The Adirondacks do exist, but the town of Silver Spring does not. However, towns that bear a resemblance to Silver Spring do exist.

Maybe you've been there.

Maybe you enjoyed it a bit too much.

And maybe you would be horrified if you discovered the histories of these towns.

Acknowledgments

Thank you, Linda Lowen, my friend and mentor, for the feedback while enjoying pizza at a restaurant that used odd naming conventions on its menu. My thanks to the Kodomo critique group for all of your valuable feedback as well.

I am grateful to Michael Dahlquist for your support and guidance with the process.

I'd like to express my gratitude to James at goonwrite.com for the amazing cover, and to Steve Passouris of bookow.com for making formatting accessible.

PART ONE

Fellow Travelers

CHAPTER 1

November 2022

Madison

Madison Webster watches them through the windshield of her aged Acura, both hands wrapped around her coffee. Steam rises from her cup, warming her nose. Sunlight filters through the dirty windshield, creating a painful glare. Windshield-washer fluid is just one more thing that will have to wait. She presses her hands tighter, absorbing the heat from her cup, waiting for the right moment to venture out into the cold.

A woman sits in the green Kia parked in the row ahead of her. Madison sees the top of a child's winter hat, pink puffball bobbing animatedly in the passenger seat. Madison tries to sip her coffee, but it's too hot. Ahead of her, the woman emerges from the driver's seat and stretches, then opens the passenger door. The child in a generic pink jacket hurries out, dancing side to side and rubbing her hands together before gripping her mother's hand. The two rush across the parking lot to the convenience store-McDonald's hybrid.

Madison knows their routines. She has seen it repeat for the past three mornings. She can set her watch by them, if she wore one anymore.

Madison checks her phone and signs. It's getting late. Quarter to nine in the morning. Time to make her move. She gulps at the still-too-hot-for-comfort coffee and grabs her oversized Michael Kors handbag. She pauses for a moment, bracing herself for the cold before pushing the door open. She pulls her hands into the sleeves of her lavender jacket, crossing her arms over her chest to conserve body heat, and walks briskly to the door of the fast-food restaurant.

Her mouth waters at the smell of an assembly line of powdered egg, meat and cheese sandwiches mixed with cheap coffee. Woven into the texture of scents, she inhales a whiff of butter and syrup that will drown someone's morning pancakes. She puts a hand over her stomach to calm the angry gnawing inside.

I can't believe I'm craving this garbage.

A line has already formed at the counter. Two men in neon yellow vests over their bulky sweatshirts and hunting jackets. A younger man, knit cap pulled low on his head, glances nervously at the menu. He shifts his weight side to side, rubbing his hands together to warm up.

Madison hovers a polite distance from the restroom door, anticipating the moment the mother and daughter will exit and she will take their place.

When they walk past her, the child looks up, a shy smile revealing two missing teeth. The girl waves, a look of recognition in her eyes. Her hair is neatly combed, no longer tangled. Madison smiles and waves back, trying to ignore the stabbing in her heart. Wondering if the Tooth Fairy ever visited that little girl.

Madison catches the restroom door with her elbow before it closes. The candy-orange scent of generic fast food restroom cleaners is her reward for getting here early, but she remains wary. The smell of cleaner and the state of cleanliness are not the same.

She checks the four stalls and finds the least foul. The balancing act begins. Madison shifts from one foot to the other, trying not to touch the walls. A dance she's almost mastered. Don't touch the walls, don't step on the floor in socks or bare feet, and don't let the Michael Kohrs rub against anything gross. She manages to change her clothes without breaking the rules.

She packs her dirty clothes tightly into a plastic bag and presses it to the bottom of her shoulder bag. She's still the only one in the bathroom, but her guilty conscience compels her to tap the toilet's handle with her foot, causing it to flush for effect.

Pushing her luck, she looks over both shoulders as she washes her hands. The coast clear still, she lets the water pool in her cupped hands and splashes the water over her face, and then her head. She leans down as close to the faucet as possible, to wash her new DIY pixie cut. Out of shampoo for now, the water alone will do. She rubs her hands through what's left of her hair, wiping away the excess water, and then grabs a paper towel to pat herself dry.

Or to look less drenched.

It's acceptable to appear recently showered this early, but public bathroom showered is never a good look.

She tries not to remember the feeling of steam rising around her, the luxury of a ten-minute shower. Her roommate, Carolyn's voice chiding her for the third-degree burns trailing down her back.

Tries not to think of Carolyn.

The door to the restroom opens. A woman heads to the nearest stall, eyes fixed on her phone, thumbs texting furiously.

Madison cringes, shakes her head, and leaves.

The restaurant is crowded now. She's once again dodged the restroom rush.

"Madison?"

She startles, heart fluttering.

No one knows me here.

She turns in the direction of the woman's voice. Madison raises a hand to her head, self-consciously patting her damp, spiky strands of honey blonde.

Oh God.

"Um, hi! It's," Madison shakes her head, "what a surprise," she stammers. She pulls her hand to her side abruptly, then jams her hands into her pockets.

She hasn't seen Jacqueline since at least Twelfth grade.

Jacqueline smiles, revealing still-perfect teeth. If she's changed at all, it's only to become more attractive. More put together.

They stare at each other for a moment before Madison blurts out, "You really look great. You haven't changed at all."

"Well, thank you! You look like you've definitely changed!" Jacqueline smiles, but Madison thinks the compliment hides an accusation.

A lump forms in her throat. Her cheeks grow warm. Inside her left pocket, she's found a straw wrapper. She fidgets with it, smoothing it between her fingers.

She knows. Of course, she knows. And everyone knows and that's why she has to go as far away as possible and pretend like…

"Your hair. Where did those wavy long locks go? How daring, looks great," Jacqueline smiles.

"Oh, oh right of course. Thanks," Madison eyes the store's exit, but her feet are frozen in place. She changes the subject. "So, what have you been up to?"

"Well," Jacqueline beams, reciting something akin to a resume. "And that's when I moved back home, because between you and me, the city just wasn't for me, but then Greg and I got married," she extends her hand, wiggling her outstretched fingers to show off her ring.

Madison smiles, eyes darting in the direction of the exit.

"And then we just bought our *second* condo before the pandemic, thank *God*! So, we've been busy fixing it up and making it feel more like home. But here I am talking about me, what about *you*?"

Madison's throat tightens. She hadn't prepared for this question, not from someone who knows her- or knew her.

"I've been, uh, traveling. A lot."

"Oh, wow. It must be so much easier being unattached. I'm jealous! We were doing mission work a few summers before the pandemic. And then last year we went to Rome and…"

Madison's salvation comes in the form of a thirty-pound child cannonball launching herself at Jacqueline, nearly knocking her to the ground.

"Mommy!" the girl pulls Jacqueline's sleeve, "Can I get a milkshake?"

Jacqueline looks down at her daughter, "Honey, yes, you can have a milkshake, just be patient while mommy…"

"Milkshake! Milkshake!" the girl chants, pulling her mother's sleeve until the fabric stretches. Jacqueline allows the child to corral her. She looks back up at Madison and shrugs, her smile resigned.

"Well, it was great running into you, I'll look for you online. Are you on TikTok?"

Madison can't think of an excuse in time. She nods, but Jacqueline has already made strides halfway to the counter, distracted by her daughter's chatter.

Just as well.

Madison looks to the ground and rushes past the morning crowd, making her way to her car. She rolls the windows down despite the chilly December air. Sleeping in the 2003 Acura is taking its toll, both on her back and on the air quality.

She pulls out of the rest stop and resumes her trip up the highway.

Of all the people, it had to be Jacqueline.

You can't outrun it.

Carolyn's voice returns to her mind.

A horn blasts, shaking Madison from the memory. Her heart turns to ice as she realizes she's drifted into the next lane, barely missing a truck. The truck pulls around her, driver leaning on the horn again and screaming something out his window.

Fair enough.

Eyes glued to the road ahead, she feels around the passenger seat for another energy drink, but only finds empty cans.

CHAPTER 2

Madison was prepared to make frequent stops along the way. No need to rush, especially in the winter, when the snowy Adirondacks can be unpredictable. She doesn't take chances. Not after what happened to her father.

The sky dims to muted blue and grey, she squints, reading the signs on the side of the highway.

Chipotle.

Subway.

Another mile fades into the distance in the rearview mirror before she finds what she is looking for.

She pulls into the Walmart, part of a plaza of big-box stores that render one city indistinguishable from the next. Michael Kors bag over her shoulder, she wanders through the store, stopping to eye a bag of chips, then a box of crackers, ultimately bypassing the grocery aisle and heading for the restroom.

Later, as she leaves the fluorescent lighting and elevator music for the silent grey evening, the security guard smiles and wishes her a good night. She thanks him. The automatic doors slide apart. She braces herself, hugging her arms against the cold.

Madison crosses the threshold, red flashing lights cut through the grey landscape. Her heart stops. She is frozen in place. The police car slows as it passes her. She holds her breath, releasing it again only as the patrol car drives by. She watches it continue to the edge of the lot. Two officers get out of the vehicle and begin knocking on windows of three cars parked along the back row of spots.

"Keep it moving. You can't stay here," one officer yells.

Her hands are numb from the cold, but she's transfixed as the sound of the officer's voice carries across the parking lot. "This ain't a hotel, keep it moving."

Madison blinks back tears, finding the motivation to hurry toward her car as if the words had been directed at her.

In a way, they were

The cold air makes her nose run. She reaches in her pocket for a tissue, or a napkin. Finding none, she pulls the cuff of her sweat-shirt through the sleeve of her jacket and holds her wrist to her nose, sniffling, the air stinging her throat.

Madison ducks into the Acura slamming the door shut as if it were a buffer between herself and a predator. In the rearview mirror, she sees the patrol car leave the parking lot, flashing lights now turned off.

She pushes her Michael Kors onto the passenger seat and starts the car, not waiting for it to warm up before returning to the highway in search of the next shopping plaza.

* * *

In less than an hour, Madison finds a nearly identical plaza. Home Depot, Wendy's Wal Mart. She hides her car in the far corner of the parking lot, choosing anonymity over the glow of the store's lighting and free Wi-Fi.

"Always so worried about what people think of you," Carolyn's voice chastises her.

You're not in my life anymore, remember?

Her rebuttal ends abruptly as she notices the car parked a few spaces away. A figure in the driver's seat, maybe another woman, eyes her from the window.

Madison turns away, face warm with embarrassment.

I don't care what anybody thinks, she whispers to Carolyn, who isn't even here.

Madison hangs a t-shirt over her window forming a makeshift curtain. She recalls an evening, weeks ago, parked near a store in Kingston. At the time, she thought she would be safer secluded in a dark corner rather than parked among the cars. But this illusion was broken when, at two in the morning, she was awakened by rapping on her window. She startled awake to find a man with white hair and a Patagonia jacket. In her confusion, she thought he must be a store manager or security guard. She still feels nauseas recalling how she rolled her window down just slightly, and how his eyes darted from side to side as he said, "I only have an hour, how much?"

She shakes the memory from her mind. Madison can see her breath and the hairs inside her nose are going numb. She wraps another blanket around her shoulders, then huddles under the foil blanket.

CHAPTER 3

Madison is used to waking every few hours to run the engine when the temperature in the car drops into the thirties. Once, she let it drop further, but her feet went numb, and she heard Carolyn's voice calling her foolish.

With shaking hands, she turns on the engine for a few minutes, but only a few.

Can't waste gas.

She blows into her hands and wraps herself in blankets. A line of red across the sky tells her she's survived another night. Dawn's maroon fingers turn orange, then gold, reaching from the horizon, she knows warmth will come if she can just wait a little longer.

Her stomach growls. She cups her hands and blows into her palms and her breath comes out in vapors she can see. She rubs her hands together.

This is all wrong.

She reaches to pat at the spikes of her hair, but then returning her hands together, trying to stay warm.

A car door closes in the distance and Madison turns to see a woman and child walking toward the Walmart entrance. The child cries and lifts their arms in the air. She hears the mother groan as she bends down to pick up the child and continue walking.

She shivers, pulls the blankets tighter, and thinks back to her childhood, and how often she and her mother skated on the razor's edge of this life after her father died.

It wouldn't have been so bad if they never lived in the bungalow on Willow Estates, a quiet, tree-lined street in the Hudson Valley. She recalls the backyard, where she sat on that spring day, entranced by the whirring of a weedwhacker in Mr. Khan's yard next door. For a moment, the whirring stopped. He mumbled a curse, and she watched the tallest of the sunflowers fall limp on the white wooden fence, before sinking down to its eternal resting place beyond her view. Gone. Before summer even had a chance to arrive. That's how quickly everything changed.

A shadow passes before her, and Madison blinks the memory away. More people vacate their cars, stretch, or huddle, and rush toward the store for a morning bathroom break.

A tear rolls down her cheek, thawing a path on her cold skin. She stares out across the parking lot. Like the people waking in their cars this morning, it could have gone another way. Carolyn, an avid sci-fi reader, used to talk about parallel universes where other trains of reality go on, mirroring our lives, but not the same.

In Madison's parallel universe, she has another life. One without the accident.

Accident.

How can something so consequential have the same word as orange juice spilled on the kitchen floor?

This is all wrong.

In the parallel universe, she would have had a better start, and she would be in an apartment- no a house- by now, and not starring as an extra in Dawn of the Living Squatters in a Wal Mart parking lot.

She sighs. Reconstructing history is exhausting. Even if it is all true in a parallel universe, it's not the way things worked out in this world. No one survived the edger.

But unlike the people here, she was called for an interview yesterday. A step down, but something. This will be temporary.

CHAPTER 4

On the road by ten the next morning, Madison flips radio stations aimlessly, her choices ranging from gospel to ten shades of country. She blinks at the monotonous mountain scenery as the Northway stretches before her. The Adirondacks are pretty. In the summer, she'd gone camping at a lodge in the mountains with friends. And in the fall, they would visit Lake Placid and stroll through town, dropping into quaint shops and enjoying a gelato.

She shivers at the thought of eating an iced treat any time other than summer.

Maybe another year, maybe two, and she would be able to return to the Golden Arrow or one of the resorts she enjoyed in the past. Private beach with white sands, clear crystal lake. Belgian waffles for breakfast.

That was the better life her college degree was supposed to bring. But rather than a talisman against poverty and ticket to the middle class, it proved useless during the recession. Each month, student loan notices would come in the mail, long after her company downsized. One dead-end job after another took her farther than the short-lived upward mobility she was just getting used to. Until finally, even those opportunities began drying up.

She turns the radio off. The reception is weaker on this stretch of highway, and nothing good on the radio anyway.

She'll need a rest stop soon. A sign marks exit 36. She doesn't want to take a detour. She's almost there. But if she doesn't go now, it could be an hour before she reaches another exit. And there is no sense in taking risks.

The exit leads to a winding road, unfolding onto Route 42.

There should be a Stewart's around here or something.

The road is longer than she expected before she comes to any sign of a commercial area. It's quaint, like those pockets of small-town revival in the region. She eyes the shops, making a mental note to stop in and visit, then another mental note that no, she won't.

She may never have the chance to just go shopping again. To buy something luxurious. A novelty. Something to bring home and laugh about during a party or game night or...

By the time she sees the figure, it's too late.

Terrified, her blood turns to ice. She opens her mouth to scream, "Get out of the way," but nothing comes out.

The woman on the edge of the road at an intersection of four corners. Her long gown is the color of apricots. Around her head, a crown of leaves, pinecones, and flowers. She stares directly into Madison's eyes.

And doesn't move.

Help! I can't stop the car!

She thinks, *Oh my God, No!*

And as her head thuds against the steering wheel, she is barely conscious of her final thought- her father, the sight of the tallest sunflower going limp, then disappearing over a fence.

CHAPTER 5

A familiar smell makes Madison smile. Someone is baking bread.
She knows it can't be her mother.
Mom will be at work whether it is early morning or evening.
Is it Carolyn? I never knew Carolyn liked baking.

* * *

The first thing she feels, before her eyes are open, is the heat from the sun on her face. Mixing with her fading dream, she imagines a nearby oven.
Don't get too close.
These thoughts fade as Madison opens her eyes. November sunlight streaming through a window lined with frost. Lace-trimmed sheer curtains. A pink canopy floats above her head, she traces the path of delicate bedposts.
A unicorn bed, she thinks, noticing the ample piles of pillows surrounding her. She tries to turn, but her neck is stuck. Pain sears her forehead…
Her face warms, and now it's on fire.
She closes her eyes.
"Carolyn," she winces at the sound of her own voice, "you got any Tylenol? I had too much to drink," she murmurs the words. Carolyn will never hear.
A strobe light white and silver, flashes behind her eyes.
Her neck hurts. It must be from being bunched up in the front seat of her car, she thinks. But as her eyes open, she sees the canopy overhead. Not the roof of her car. She slips back into darkness.

CHATER 6

In the dream, Madison walks through an unfamiliar house. A cat hangs around her neck. Its fur is itchy, the cat is heavy, and unmovable. She carries him like an albatross from room to room.

Carolyn follows behind her.

"Looks like your kind of place. Was it worth it?"

"Don't give me that shit," Madison turns to confront her friend.

The room is empty. It's a study lined with books she means to read as soon as she has the time. Things have been so busy at the advertising firm. But she has a vacation coming up, eventually.

She tries for a closer view of the spines of one of the books but the more she strains the blurrier her vision.

Too much screen time.

And there is the piano. Just like she used to play in middle school, when she visited her cousin's house. She means to get back to it. Someday.

The hallway is empty.

She heads for the kitchen, suddenly thirsty. The cat- what was his name anyway- bears down with his weight and she feels him crushing the small bones stacked on her spine.

She approaches the fridge and reaches for some tea. Madison unscrews the cap and begins drinking from the bottle, tea pouring down her chin. She tries to tip her head back farther but the cat protests, digging his claws into her neck.

"I'm putting you on a diet," she tells the cat.

Piano music echoes through the room. She can't name the song but it's familiar. Her aunt is obsessed with some old band called the Beatles. She rolls her eyes.

The music speeds up. Then slows down.

A voice carries down the hall now, singing along with the tune in words she can't make out.

Madison puts the empty bottle on the counter and wipes tea from her chin. She's spilled it down her neck.

What the hell is wrong with you?

Something is wrong with the music. It was fine a minute ago, and now the piano sounds out of tune. Slower. Carolyn plays it in a new key, the sound ominous.

Chills pass over Madison's bones.

Was Carolyn playing a prank?

Madison reaches to dislodge the cat's nails from her neck. She feels herself clapped between two boards. Something hard and stabbing. Two walls crushed together.

Or an airbag and the seat of a car…

It's December. She sees it now. The four corners. Afternoon sun fading. The figure standing by the road.

Hears herself scream, "Watch out!" As she loses control of the car.

Hears the music, and someone, not Carolyn, singing.

Her heart freezes in her chest.

She wakes gasping for air and her lungs weighed down from pain in her back. Piano music is distant, no longer an eerie distorted key. There is no cat around her neck, only a brace. Her hair and sweaty shoulders itch. The remnants of a migraine linger behind her eyes.

And a woman old enough to be her mother stands by her bed, eclipsing the view of the ornate doll house.

"Relax, you're okay. Didn't mean to startle you," the woman smiles. "I'm Billie Jo." The woman in the doorway has long blonde hair and a warm, kind face. Madison thinks if the stranger was an actor, she would be typecast as the glamorous yet highly efficient soccer mom who somehow finds time to make brownies for the school bake sale while working out and managing a list of fascinating hobbies.

Where am I?

Madison tries to piece together fragments of a dream, memory, and fantasy and can't discern where the edges begin and end.

"Where? What happened? Is that woman with the crown okay?"

Billie Jo squints, her face concerned and confused. "You had a little accident."

I wet the bed? Madison wonders, but before she can check, her host explains.

"You crashed your car. Don't worry. You'll be okay. Just need some rest."

Madison's relief is short-lived as she remembers the figure at the four corners. Her heart races, she needs to know but is afraid to ask.

"There was someone there. Did I hit her? Is she dead?" Her words come out in desperate gasps now as her breath becomes shallow.

Billie Jo looks at her, face comforting and concerned, "Oh, sweetie, don't you worry. There was no one at the scene, dear. You might have bumped your head. Only one hurt was you and you're going to be fine."

Madison tries to steady her breathing, relieved. Yes. It was a mirage, or a vision, or one of those weird things that happen with concussions. Another thought occurs to her.

My car. I need my car. I live in my car.

She doesn't speak the words aloud, still struggling to catch her breath. Trying to make sense of what this woman is telling her.

"My car?" She finally manages.

"It'll be fine. Just going to take a few days for parts to come in. Supply chain and all," she says the last part confidentially as if she is letting Madison in on a nod to some conspiracy. "But my brother is the mechanic, he'll take care of it for you."

"Do I have broken bones? Have I been to a hospital?"

"No, honey, no need for all that. Dr. Needham stopped by yesterday when we brought you home. Checked you all out from here. You'll be fine. You just need to rest."

Madison sank deeper into the bed, registering the words. No one was hurt. Just her. But the woman in the gown and leaves around her head? Had she imagined her?

"Did you say a doctor came here?"

"Yes, Dr. Needham."

"He does house calls? That's unusual. Isn't it?"

Billie Jo's expression doesn't change. "Not at all. He's been doing it for twenty years and his father before him and his grandfather before that."

Madison should be relieved but still feels hesitant.

"He left some medicine for you. A tincture. For the pain. You can have some again in a few hours. I'll bring it up with your soup. But for now, you just try to relax."

The piano starts again. It's coming from downstairs she realizes now. Not the Beatles. Why had she thought it was the Beatles? It's Air on a G String.

"My daughter, Emily, plays the piano. She thought you might want some music. Help you relax." Billie Jo smiles.

Madison returns the smile though her eyes hurt when she does. "It's beautiful. She's talented, please tell her thank you."

"Oh, she's talented all right. Successful, about to be married in a few weeks," Billie Jo beams as she says this, "now my other one, Desirae, well," the woman leans in as if sharing a secret, "there's one in every family."

The older woman smiles, rolling her eyes. Madison doesn't follow but she smiles too. Suddenly overwhelmed, her eyelids heavy. She feels herself lowered into sleep, lulled by the music, and by the time she dreams again, the opening notes to Yesterday seep deep into her subconscious.

CHAPTER 7

Madison has lost track of how many days have passed while she drifted in and out of sleep. For a moment she thinks the woman, Billie Jo, was just another bizarre dream. But as her eyes adjust, she sees the pink decorations. Feels the ruffled blankets of the unicorn bed. Turns to see the wooden doll house.

She remembers in fragments.

Car accident, her car is in the shop. She's somewhere in the Adirondacks. It's winter. Carolyn will start to worry, except she won't worry because they haven't spoken since the falling out.

Her head spins.

She wants to go back to sleep and wake up when it is over.

But I have a job interview…

Her heart sinks. By the time this is over, she realizes the job won't be available. Her head sears with pain as reality catches up with her.

She wants to pull one of the frilly spare pillows over her face and scream but pain won't let her. She suddenly wishes her friend was here. The room feels too big. The world is too empty. Her heart races as the feeling of being completely untethered sinks in.

A movement in the doorway distracts her.

"Hello?" she groans, her voice weak.

A teen lingers, peeking in at her, a look of disdain on her face.

"Hey," the shadow in the doorway pushes the door open and peers in. Madison guesses the child is fourteen or fifteen. "Almost dinner, if you want to come downstairs." The invitation sounds forced. The child's eyes are distant, expression flat.

"Uhm, no, I don't think I can," she hasn't thought about food until now and the idea makes her nauseous. "Thanks, though."

The girl's clothes don't match, and her haircut looks self-induced. This can't be Emily, the piano player.

"What day is it?"

"It's Thursday."

Madison has been in bed for two days. The interview is over. Her pain and nausea give way to a sinking feeling. Like the ground caving in beneath her.

"My car? Do you know where my phone is?" she has no one to call but feels apart from the world without the internet.

Before the girl can answer, Billie Jo appears in the doorway. "Are you bothering our guest?" she asks.

The girl slips out of Madison's view. "No," she answers before disappearing.

"I'm sorry, that's Desirae, my youngest. She has no manners."

"It's okay, really."

"Would you like me to bring you a plate? You haven't eaten in days." Billie Jo looks concerned. Madison is touched. What is this place?

"Thanks, but I still feel pretty sick."

"Maybe just some tea and crackers," Billie Jo nods her head and says this in a gentle but assured way. Madison doesn't argue. Moments later the woman returns. Madison tries to sit up in bed, but her head swims and she can only manage to prop herself up on pillows. Good enough, she sips the tea. Lemon, mint, and ginger soothe her.

"Thank you. I really appreciate it. I'll be out of your hair as soon as my car is ready."

"You'll do no such thing." Billie Jo's abrupt tone startles Madison. The older woman sits at the foot of the bed.

Madison's eyes widen, she suddenly feels trapped. She tries to look around for an escape but can't keep her eyes off the woman at the foot of the bed.

Billie Jo continues, "You're welcome to stay as long as you want. We're all family here."

Madison smiles as far as she can before her headache causes her to wince.

"You look about the same size as my Emily. I found some of her old clothes in the attic, help yourself to whatever you like."

Billie Jo gestures to a neatly folded pile of clothes on a small table. "Thanks."

"Get as much rest as you need. You can stay as long as you like."

Madison thinks she saw the woman wink, but her vision clears. She's smiling, that's all. Billie Jo leaves her alone again. The knot in her stomach subsides.

I can get used to this.

When she next drifts to sleep, Madison sees the girl again, Desirae. She stands in the doorway, staring silently. Madison turns her head to the side and is surprised to see Jacqueline, her old frenemy, sitting in an ornate chair glancing at the doll house.

"We bought one just like it, "Jacqueline tells her without turning to face the bed. "We have three, actually."

She watches as Jacqueline rearranges furniture in the wooden house. She picks up a pair of gardening shears and begins cutting the tiny wooden furniture, then sweeps the pieces onto the floor.

When she's finished, she stands back and extends her hand as if to say behold, a masterpiece. Madison, now fully awake, sits up in bed, it doesn't hurt now. She hears a noise. Squeaking.

Is it my car?

She looks closer in time to see a large brown rat shimmy out from the dollhouse, slide down the dresser, and stalk across the floor in her direction.

Chapter 8

Madison's body aches. She rubs the back of her neck, moving slowly as she descends the stairs, wearing a loose-fitting western-inspired top and jeans from the clothes that were once Emily's. She's used to wearing the clothes other girls discarded. It was a normal routine after her father died. She used to hate taking charity. Before her father died, she always had new clothes to start the school year. But in her sophomore year, she wore an outfit that had gone out of style years earlier. Even washed, it retained the scent of someone else's closet, a constant reminder it wasn't hers.

She remembers her first job out of college, she bought a new outfit and paid so much for it she was afraid to wear it, something Carolyn teased her about.

But wearing Emily's clothes feels different. Not a mark of shame, but as a token of acceptance she can't fully understand.

She holds a hand over her left eye, blocking out the worst of the glare from the hallway light, her head still sore from the crash.

She follows the din of light chatter down a hall to a dining room. It's simple yet comfortable. Family photos line the walls and several generations sit around the table. She recognizes Billie Jo at the head of the table and an elderly woman at the other end. Desirae looks her up and down and closes her eyes, but not before letting out a disgruntled moan.

"Welcome, Madison! Have a seat."

Billie Jo gestures to an empty chair to her right. Madison smiles, then hesitates. She doesn't remember telling the older woman her name. Then again, if her brother is the town mechanic, he may have found her ID in the car.

Madison slides into the chair and keeps her eyes down, stifling her anxiety about where her bag ended up and the anxiety percolating with the myriad of unasked questions.

Billie Jo distracts her from worrying. The woman looks radiant with hospitable excitement, she gestures to a man with salt and pepper hair and a round face. His rosy cheeks give him a perpetually cheery look. Billie Jo begins introductions.

"This is my husband, Mark."

Mark smiles and nods slightly in a shy greeting. His face seems young, giving him the appearance of a child with greying hair.

"And my mother, we all call her Grandma Winnie."

Madison smiles at the elderly woman. She wears age well, her hair silver rather than dull and grey. She gives a brief nod to acknowledge Madison. Unlike Billie Jo, Grandma Winnie keeps her expression stoic, as if she's lived long enough to see strangers come and go from the dinner table and nothing fazes her. Not even a stray who nearly mauled a strange woman dressed in a crown of leaves before ending up seated amidst her family.

"You already met Desirae," Billie Jo's voice is dismissive as she points out the presence of her younger child.

"And this is my daughter Emily, and her fiancée, Glen," Billie Jo continues.

Emily looks like a younger clone of her mother, Madison thinks.

"Thank you for letting me borrow your clothes," Madison smiles, feeling awkward.

"It's my pleasure," Emily's face is warm, and kind, just like her mother's. One hand on her glass, the glint of diamonds catches Madison's eye. Glen has good taste, she thinks, noticing the prominent diamonds. Yet it's elegant, not gaudy.

"Glen just proposed on Thanksgiving," Emily explains. Madison blushes, realizing she must have been staring.

"Because I'm so thankful for you, my princess," Glen puts an arm around Emily, grinning ear to ear.

They're a perfect couple, Madison thinks. Cute, slightly nauseating. The kind that can make you both jealous and hopeful.

"I have an idea," Billie Jo claps her hands together as she smiles, somehow wider than before. Her eyes are bright as if she's been struck by some epiphany. She turns to Madison, "Why don't you join Emily and me tomorrow? We're shopping for dresses for the bride's maids. It will be so much fun!"

Emily smiles, mirroring her mother's excitement.

"You girls have fun, I'm keeping my distance," Glen jokes, looking to Mark for reassurance.

Madison doesn't want to sound ungrateful, but her shoulders still ache, and her head throbs.

"I'm honored," Madison chooses her words carefully, "Still a little sore, though. I don't want to slow you down."

"Oh, don't worry about that," Emily waves her hand, dismissing Madison's words. "We won't be in any rush. And I can get you some of the good stuff from Dr. Needham if Tylenol isn't strong enough." Emily winks.

Madison doesn't know what to say, but she has a feeling that if she doesn't accept the invitation, she'll seem rude.

"Oh, well, thanks. That would be fun."

"Yay!" Emily claps her hands.

The door behind Madison opens and a woman enters, bearing trays of food.

Everyone is silent. No one introduces this family member and it's only when she places steaming plates of chicken, quinoa, and assorted vegetables on the table and retreats from the room that Madison realizes she must be a servant. Or maid? What is the word these days?

Madison's skin prickles. She looks around the room, trying to find a way to break the silence. Her eyes settle on the youngest family member.

"Desirae, are you coming too?"

The girl meets her gaze. To Madison's surprise, Desirae's eyes are brimming with anger. Madison's face grows warm as she realizes she may have stumbled into a concealed family resentment. An only child, she had periodically been surprised when other families presented their intricate sibling rivalries.

Desirae replies in a low voice, "I don't indulge in patriarchal bullshit."

Mark slams a hand on the table, "Desirae, what did we say about that?"

He turns to Madison, "I'm sorry, my daughter is rude and doesn't know how to act in front of company."

Billie Jo continues, "Desirae is going through her teenage phase. She'll grow out of it. Someday she'll look back and be mortified by some of her choices."

Madison understands. She feels something like pity for the child, but also disdain. Desirae has both parents and a grandmother. A home with a piano, and photos on the walls, and even a servant. Or maid. Or domestic helper. Where does she get off being so miserable?

"Madison, eat up, help yourself to anything you want, you must be starving." Billie Jo nudges a plate of rosemary chicken closer to her.

"Thank you. Sorry, I spaced out for a minute." She begins tentatively selecting from the trays, careful not to eat to satiety, not wanting anyone to know how hungry she has really been.

No need to make them suspicious.

Madison reaches for a fork, but there are several. She read an article once about fancy restaurants and the correct silverware to use for each part of a meal. She and Carolyn read it together. They laughed, she remembers, and Carolyn even made a funny voice that she called her Mrs. Worthington voice. From that point on, any time they wanted to refer to a pretentious person, Carolyn would slip into Mrs. Worthington, sitting up straight, holding her pinky out, and donning the fake prep-school voice.

Staring at the silverware, Madison wishes she paid more attention to the article, rather than making fun of it. She eyes Billie Jo, noticing the woman is using a medium-sized fork, and mimics her host.

CHAPTER 9

Walking around the bedroom the following morning, Madison takes in her surroundings. A bulletin board above an old wooden desk covered with photos taken in high school. She recognizes Emily in a Halloween costume, dressed as Glinda the Good Witch. Beside her, she sees a much younger Desirae dressed not as Dorothy, but as the Tin Man. Not the Wicked Witch of the West? She thinks, a smirk forming on her face. In the photo, Desirae holds a Yorkie Madison assumes was a Toto that Halloween.

Beside the Halloween photo, another picture of Emily in a cheerleader's uniform, and another surrounded by girls grinning proudly at an award ceremony.

Several Medals hang from the wall. First place in track, a prize from a piano competition, and another marked "Little Miss Silver Spring, 1997."

She wonders what it was like growing up in Silver Spring. She imagines sitting on the frilly unicorn bed late into the evening, talking on a phone, with a chord, old-school. Gossipping to friends about boys and teachers. Looking up at the canopy and giggling into the ample throw pillows. She imagines Billie Jo knocking on the door to say "it's getting late, dear. Come down for dinner. You need your beauty sleep for cheerleading tomorrow."

A brief knock brings her back to the present. Emily peeks into the room, "Are you ready for shopping?" Emily raises here eyebrows on the word 'shopping' as if it is the most enticing prospect in the small town.

Madison's stomach turns, she tries to stifle her reaction, forcing her face into a smile. Shopping hasn't been a treat in a long time.

"Yes, sorry, didn't mean to be nosy, I was just admiring your room. You know," Madison begins to say *It's the kind I always dreamt about having if things were different…* but stops herself. She thinks of Ms. Jeffries' improv class at acting camp.

"You are free to build the role," she used to say. "So, draw on what you know of human nature, but don't constrain yourself by following what has been true for you. You are acting. You are improvising. So, make it believable, but make it up."

Madison sees that Emily is watching her, waiting for her to finish her sentence, she smiles and continues, "You know, I was just thinking, this is almost exactly what my bedroom was like when I was growing up."

"Really?" Emily giggles.

Madison nods, getting into character, "Yes, only my bed, we used to call it the unicorn bed, it had a pink and purple bedspread, but also a canopy like yours. And," she looks side to side confidentially and leans closer to Emily, "I had horrible taste in boybands so there were a few posters on the wall that are, let's say, regrettable."

They both laugh. "But I don't want to make you late for your big day, I just have to get my shoes on." She scans the room, then remembers she doesn't know where her shoes are. Before she can ask, Emily interrupts her, "Ah, yes, that reminds me," the woman ducks into the hallway, opens a closet, retrieving her shoes from a shelf along with something bulky. Her bag.

"Mom said these were in your car."

Emily places the bag and shoes on the table. Madison's first urge is to check her bag to make sure everything is still there, but she stops herself.

Heat forms on her face. She avoids Emily's gaze.

Why would this family steal from her?

Madison puts on her shoes and slings the bag over her shoulder. She takes a deep breath. Shopping, she tells herself, can be fun. She doesn't have to buy anything. It can be social. Like in high school. She follows Emily down the stairs.

Madison is the last out the door. "Um, I don't think the door is locked?" She calls after her host, rushing to catch up.

Billie Jo stands by the SUV, ready to open the door for Grandma Winnie. All three women turn to Madison with confused, patronizing looks.

"Lock the door?" Billie Jo laughs, "Honey, we don't lock doors in Silver Spring."

"No?"

"Of course not. We don't have crime. We don't even have police."

"Really?" Madison's eyes are wide. She's never heard of a place where people don't lock their doors and thought not having police was one of Carolyn's pipe dreams.

"Nope. Haven't needed police since before my time. We all share the same values. It works out better that way."

Billie Jo winks as she says this. Madison is sure this time.

* * *

The winter sunlight is sharp and abrasive, piercing through the windows of Billie Jo's SUV. Madison contemplates asking Emily about the more potent medicine as her head is still spinning. Madison can't resist watching out the passenger window with fascination as they pass through the streets of the storybook town.

It snowed since her arrival, but the sidewalks and roads are clear. The snow is clean, just enough for decoration, not so much as to be a nuisance, it coats the curbs and branches of trees lining the streets. Modest but well-kept cape and Victorian style houses line the residential neighborhoods, children pull a sled down along a path, a puppy chasing after them. Even the Main Street buildings are quaint, charming, perfect.

Emily outlines the agenda for the day from her front passenger seat, Madison's mind drifts, she hears words from a song she can't fully recall, about a place where it never rained until after sundown.

The memory crystallizes slowly. The song was from Camelot, the musical, performed by her high school. Jacqueline, of course, played Guinevere. She was one of the anonymous chorus members which she later understood meant backdrop. It was fun at the time, nevertheless. And this place, Silver Spring, this must be Camelot, weather tamed into perfection codified, every house obediently playing its part in setting the scene for a Hallmark Christmas movie, if there should ever be one filmed here.

She is lost in thought when she notices something odd. Standing apart from the Christmas displays and twinkling lights wrapped around the lamp posts on Main Street. Apart from the figures dressed in business casual, walking purposefully from store to post office to cars. A figure leaning against the wall of a corner convenience store.

Madison notices the woman's bare arms first.

She must be freezing.

The dress, long and flowing, the color of apricots. The woman's head is crowned with bright orange leaves and pinecones.

Madison gasps.

"I know, right?" Emily responds, "Rose gold is in this season, I think it's a much better decision than teal."

Emily's voice pulls Madison's attention back into the car only for a moment, but when she returns her gaze, the woman is gone.

Madison recovers control of her breathing. She doesn't want to change the subject and plays along as if she was listening the whole time, "Yes, it's beautiful."

"Thank you!"

Madison can see Emily grinning through her reflection in the side mirror. The bride-to-be continues, "I kept trying to tell Arianna, but she is partial to teal. But teal will never do in July. Maybe a February wedding, but not July."

"Teal is nice for a fall bride," Madison offers, the woman in the apricot dress still on her mind.

Emily and Billie Jo exchange glances, then Emily looks at Madison, her eyes stern, as if she's committed some fashion offense.

"No, dear," Emily's voice is patronizing, her face betrays a look of alarm. "You don't want to wish for a fall wedding."

This never occurred to Madison. Among her friends, October weddings were trendy. But this is the Adirondacks. Maybe the weather is too cold by October here. She drops the subject.

Grandma Winnie, silent previously, chimes in from her seat beside Madison, "Your wedding will be perfect, honey. Try to enjoy the big day. Don't fret about every detail. You only marry once," she smiles then adds, "You're not from Greenridge, so you better only marry once."

For some reason, the family finds this funny and erupts into laughter. Madison isn't sure she follows the joke but plays along and laughs, nonetheless.

Emily is still talking about wedding plans when they pull up alongside a three-story refurbished building. The sign reads Malinda's Bridal Salon.

Madison wants to ask why they are at a salon, self-consciously touching the soft hairs growing back in. She's due for a shave, she thinks. Then again, I have a place to stay with indoor plumbing, she reminds herself.

For how long? Carolyn's voice chides.

Madison ignores the voice. She follows the women into what turns out to be a dress shop like nothing she's ever seen. The lights are dim, but mannequins adorned with gowns stand sentinel on pillars, illuminated by spotlights. Soft music plays in the background, the lyrics are light and bubbly. She doesn't pay attention to the words, focusing instead on the dazzling sights. Throughout the store are cream and white leather sofas with glass tables. Pitchers of water with assorted fruit and mock wine glasses as well as chocolates are on display. She wonders if you can just sit and eat and drink. She wonders who would dare touch chocolate in a store like this.

Emily grabs her elbow and whisks her in the direction of the bridesmaid gowns. Madison's nerves twinge at the sudden motion, but the gesture of intimacy and excitement makes her smile. Here she is. In Camelot. With a kind host family, planning a wedding. Like one of the girls.

CHAPTER 10

Madison is walking on air that evening when she returns to the room she now thinks of as hers. And why not? Grandma Winnie and Billie Jo referred to it that way more than once.

You don't belong here, Carolyn's voice creeps into her mind.

Of course, Carolyn would try to ruin a good time like this, Madison thinks. She ignores the voice.

You need to leave.

She rolls her eyes. No hurry to leave, where is her car anyway? And nowhere to go. Madison asked Billie Jo about how she can help around the house, to pull her weight while she's in town.

"That's why we have a servant," Billie Jo replied.

"I appreciate your generosity. If there's anything you need help with let me know. I'm a graphic designer, I mean I can help with that, if you need it?"

Billie Jo only smiled, "When the time comes for you to help, you'll know."

Sinking onto the bed, Madison recalls the highlight of the day. Emily, realizing one of her bridesmaids couldn't make it after all, asked Madison to stand in as a surrogate. The dressing room at the Bridal store- Salon- she reminds herself, was bigger than her bedroom.

And here she is, turning and posing before three-way mirrors, modeling a rose gold gown. Surrounded by new friends. New family. And to think, only a few days ago she was sleeping in her car.

The thought makes Madison sit upright. She forgot to check her bag. Not that she has any need to, she reminds herself. She crosses the room and turns the light back on. Reaching into her bag, she feels her wallet, a few pens, some change, the familiar feel of her clothes. She doesn't feel her keys.

Of course, because the mechanic would have them.

But something else is missing.

Her phone.

CHAPTER 11

The next morning, Madison wakes to the sound of laughter and dishes clattering. She descends the stairs to find Mark, Billie Jo, Grandma Winnie, and Emily finishing breakfast.

"Rise and shine, sleepy gal," Emily greets her.

"Good morning, sorry I slept so late. I'm lost without my phone," Madison tries to sound casual.

She waits for Billie Jo to say 'Oh, honey, I forgot all about it! My brother found it in the car,' or even 'Hmmm, what kind of phone was it? I'll keep an eye out for it.'

Instead, Mark responds, "Oh, speaking of time, I have a meeting with the Huntington firm."

He rounds the table, stoops to kiss Billie Jo on the top of her head and gives Emily a side hug.

"Maddie, have a good day and keep an eye on these two, keep them out of trouble, okay?" He winks.

She isn't sure when she became Maddie but doesn't complain.

"That's our Mark. Always wheeling and dealing," Grandma Winnie beams with pride.

Emily pats the chair beside her, inviting Maddie to sit. She's forgotten about her phone and the question dancing on the top of her head a moment ago- *why doesn't anyone here have cell phones?-* and instead pulls up the chair beside Emily.

The silent woman bustles in from the door Maddie assumes leads to the kitchen, trays in hand. She clears Mark's plate and refreshes glasses of orange juice, pouring a fresh glass for Maddie.

"Thank you," Maddie says out of habit, noticing no one else addresses the woman. Her departure is as fast as her arrival.

"Eat up, we can't have you losing any weight now," Emily pushes a tray of eggs, bacon, and scalloped potatoes toward Maddie.

"Thank you," she giggles self-consciously at the odd statement, then asks, "So, what is your, um, housekeeper's name? She's a very good cook."

Billie Jo waves a hand dismissively, "Please, Maddie, no need for the PC stuff here, you're among friends. She's our servant and she does her job, that's all." Billie Jo sips her orange juice and continues, "all this," gesturing to the house, "this is from hard work, isn't it, Grandma Winnie?"

The family elder finishes chewing and dabs her mouth with a napkin, leaving maroon lipstick stains on the cloth. "Indeed, it is. No one could even imagine we'd make it this far." Her voice is tremulous, and she speaks slowly. She raises both hands as she says, "But now? Success beyond our wildest dreams, they say. And my Ralph, bless his soul, he didn't get to enjoy the luxury as we have it now."

"Well, he's watching down on us from Heaven, right, Mom?" Emily holds her grandmother's hand from across the table as she says this, gently squeezing in reassurance.

"Maddie, you're living with a celebrity," Billie Jo smiles coyly, eyeing Grandma Winnie.

"Really?" Maddie's eyes light up. She wonders if Grandma Winnie was a dancer or singer back in her day.

"Oh, yes. Grandma Winnie was one of the founders of Silver Spring."

Grandma Winnie smiles but Maddie notices something pass across her face and her eyes become distant. She thinks it's an old people thing and turns instead to Billie Jo.

"Grandma is the last matriarch left of the founders that tamed this wilderness and turned it into the beautiful town you see today.

"Wow, that's amazing."

"Yes, she's president of the Preservation Society, which in Silver Spring means she's more powerful than the mayor."

"And better looking," Grandma Winnie adds.

Maddie cuts a piece of bacon as Billie Jo explains, "This place is very special. We have a true community. Everyone gets along, everyone does their share, and we have no crime. Zero," to accentuate, she forms an 'o' with her thumb and index finger in a sign that used to offend Carolyn. Maddie shakes the thought away. Everything used to offend Carolyn. She wonders briefly how they managed to stay friends for so long.

The memory of her friend gives way to a more recent memory. "There's something I've been meaning to ask you. About the woman in the orange gown? I saw her right before the crash. And I saw her again yesterday on the way to the, um, salon?"

Grandma Winnie and Billie Jo exchange glances. Billie Jo sips her orange juice, as if signaling that Grandma Winnie can take this question.

"What did the person look like?"

Maddie gestured toward her head, circling her hand above her brow to improvise a headpiece, "She was wearing this crown made of leaves?"

Grandma Winnie's eyes are unreadable. Billie Jo stares at her nails as if they are fascinating.

"Must have been someone going to a party, perhaps? Sounds like nothing to worry about. There was no one hurt. No one around. You may just have hit your head and thought you saw it." Grandma Winnie dismisses her question.

Maddie isn't sure how to respond. She doesn't want to make them uncomfortable and tries to think of a new topic, but Emily comes to her rescue.

"After breakfast, I have to drop Desirae at her coach's, then downtown to do some more shopping. You should come."

"Sure," Maddie wants to point out she doesn't have money and no place to put things, at least not permanently, but she doesn't want to draw attention. So far, they haven't asked about her past. She wants to keep it that way.

"We've got great stores downtown. You're so lucky you found us," Emily puts a hand on Madison's arm as she says this, her tone sincere.

"I'm lucky, yes. Thank you for letting me stay here," and adds awkwardly, "I don't know how long I can stay, but I appreciate it."

"Not at all, we're a welcoming town. We love it when people come to stay," Billie Jo smiles, rising from the table adding, "We're just thrilled to have new blood in the town, aren't we?"

"It's not everyone's cup of tea, being this far from the big cities, but we love it," Emily replies.

"It seems like a nice, quiet place."

"Oh, it is. Perfect place to settle down and raise a family. And there's plenty of men," Emily winks, again reminding Maddie that she is the spitting image of her mother in appearance and mannerisms.

"Safest place to raise a family," Grandma Winnie pipes up, reminding Maddie she's still at the table.

"That's good to know."

"I've got to meet with the Preservation Society and then the Christmas Party Committee, but I will see you ladies back here later." Billie Jo grabs her coat and purse, but before leaving the house, she calls up the stairs, "Desirae, time for your coach, don't keep Emily waiting," Grandma Winnie pauses, eyes Maddie, and adds, "and you are to act like a *lady*. You represent this family in public."

The only response from upstairs is the thud Madison presumes is Desirae stomping down the hall.

Grandma Winnie eases herself up from the table. The server, whose name Maddie realizes she still doesn't know, rushes in and begins piling dishes high.

"What sport does Desirae play?" Maddie asks Emily, taking the cue that breakfast is over and pushing in her chair.

"Sport? Oh, no honey, the last thing she needs is to play sports. Don't put ideas in that child's head. Besides, she's not the motivated type," Emily thinks for a moment, then adds, "That's what the coach is helping her with. She's more of a mentor, to encourage Desirae to make better choices."

Maddie thinks she understands. In high school, some of her classmates' parents hired life coaches instead of therapists, willing to pay the price to avoid the stigma.

Emily turns toward the living room, calling in the direction of the stairs, "Speaking of the Devil, come on, dear, we mustn't be late."

Maddie hears Desirae's feet, hidden in chunky boots, stomping down the stairs. Madison remembers when Doc Martins were in style. Kids wore combat boots to school. They were noisy and made the short kids several inches taller. She never understood the point. Desirae is petite. Madison thinks her noisy descent is intentional, not necessary.

"Good morning," Maddie addresses the girl.

"No, really, it's not. Climate change is…"

"Not a topic of conversation when we have someplace to go," Emily pulls a jacket around her sister's shoulders and interrupts her. Madison's relieved. She knows climate change is a problem, obviously. But why complain about it at this moment? What good does it do to bring it up all the time? Especially in such a beautiful place.

Grandma Winnie points her index finger at the child, her voice impatient, "You walk- young lady," emphasis on the word lady, "up those stairs and change into your shoes. Girls' shoes, and then come down those stairs silently."

Ouch, Maddie thinks. She's known strict grandparents, but Grandma Winnie is no joke. Then again, Desirae was rude. Making so much noise. Maddie tries not to stare as the child, also avoiding everyone's gaze, walks back up the stairs and disappears down the hallway. When she re-emerges, she is wearing pink Mary Janes. More Maddie's style. But she can understand why Desirae doesn't like them.

Surveying the child head to toe, the irregular half-shaved haircut, olive and grey sweater, and jeans combined with pink shoes make Desirae look like a goth teen who robbed a cheerleader. But young people do need to learn respect. She secretly applauds Grandma Winnie for setting boundaries for Desirae's own good.

Part Two

Small Town Charm

CHAPTER 12

Maddie finds Billie Jo in the living room, peering through piles of books stacked on the glass coffee table in front of her. Billie Jo doesn't notice Maddie at first, and when she does, she looks up, startled, her shock quickly giving way to the warm smile Maddie has come to associate with love. She smiles back, eyes transfixed on the older woman who has become a surrogate mother.

"I'm sorry, I didn't mean to scare you," Maddie begins.

"Don't apologize, dear," her eyebrows furrow in a look of concern, "Is something wrong?"

Maddie isn't sure how to start the conversation. It's been weeks. She has no idea where her car or her phone is, but she doesn't want to sound ungrateful. And it's not like she has any place to go.

"I'm fine, thanks," she hesitates, "but there is something I wanted to talk to you about, but when you have time," Maddie gestures to the books, "I don't want to interrupt."

Billie Jo sits up, setting her book aside. Maddie can't see the title, the cover is worn with age.

"Now is a perfect time. I just like to go through these old books for the Preservation Society once in a while. Nothing crucial, come, sit."

She gestures to the loveseat at a right angle from the sofa and Maddie sits, leaning forward, hands gripping her knees.

"So, I've been thinking, um, I really appreciate all you are doing for me, and I love it here. I love your town, that is, and your family."

Maddie knows she's rambling. She tries to make eye contact but settles for looking just past Billie Jo's shoulder.

"I just don't want to be a burden, I was wondering, um, if I'm going to be here for a while, I was wondering if you know any place is hiring? That way I can pay rent and help out and maybe find a place in town to move into."

Maddie knows pity has a threshold. She saw the pattern play out after her father died. First her aunt, then various family friends offered charity. A spare room and promises that it was no trouble descended into resentment and strained relationships within weeks, at most a few months. Her mother shuffled from one helpful friend's spare room to another's couch between apartments.

"Oh, of course!" Billie Jo begins, Maddie can't read her expression at first. The older woman puts both hands on her forehead, a gesture of frustration, or an epiphany, Maddie can't tell. "Maddie, of course, I am so sorry, I've been so busy with the holiday party and everything, I completely forgot that you've been stuck here and have things you would like to do."

Maddie sighs, relieved. That was easy. Her car is ready; Billie Jo just forgot to tell her. She nods her head.

"How careless of me. Yes, great idea. Let's get you set up with a job and then you can really settle into the town. I'll introduce you to everyone- they'll love you- and you'll be all set."

Kind of? Maddie thinks.

She says, "Oh, sure."

Her chest tightens. She should be more direct. Ask about her car. Her phone. But she doesn't want to sound rude. And maybe those details aren't so important as long as she has something to do and a place of her own.

"Interior design, right?"

"Graphic arts."

Billie Jo's face lights up, she claps her hands together, "Well, perfect, then it's settled."

"It is?"

"Yes, of course, you can come work at the Preservation Society. They're looking for someone with your talents."

"Do I need to call for an interview?" Maddie asks again, hoping Billie Jo will get the hint and say something about her missing phone.

"Not when you're part of this family," she winks.

Maddie isn't used to this. She's never been an insider. It doesn't occur to her at first that Billie Jo doesn't have any proof of her talents. She hasn't seen her portfolio. A portfolio she has no access to without her phone.

"Let's stop in for a visit now. I'll introduce you to Ruth Ann, and it will be a done deal."

Maddie is speechless. Nothing is ever this easy. Her luck must be changing. "I don't know what to say, thank you. And I'll pay rent and board and…"

"No need. You're family dear. And we aren't using Emily's old room. She told me the other day she is so happy she met you," Billie Jo leans in confidentially, "and she's so excited you're staying in her room. That's payment enough.

Maddie can't believe this is happening.

Which should be a red flag, she hears Carolyn warning her.

Not for the first time, she ignores Carolyn.

CHAPTER 13

The weekend before Christmas, the town gathers at the Silver Spring Center Mansion, a restored 18th-century mansion that serves as an event hall for concerts, conferences, and the most upscale weddings. Maddie knows this just like she knows the names of the families who worked together to turn the building from a neglected mansion on the verge of collapse to a magnificent, palatial event space. She knows this, and a laundry list of town trivia from who built the post office- The Clementine family- to the names of the last three mayors.

Maddie has succumbed to the nickname given to her by the Harris family, no longer thinks of herself as Madison. She can hardly remember a time when she slept in her car in retail store parking lots. She has forgotten what it's like to live life attached to a cell phone and has been deconditioned from checking the internet. She is a Harris now. And it's been weeks since she heard Carolyn's voice in her mind.

The transformation is so complete, Maddie doesn't notice it. She walks down the block to work at the Preservation Society, dines with the Harris family, and trades town gossip with Emily and her friends. It doesn't occur to her she once had a life outside Silver Spring.

Tonight, for the Christmas party, Maddie traded her bulky shoulder bag for a tiny purse to match her green velour dress. Her hair is growing back in spiky tufts which she tamed into submission with a rosy-scented gel. She and Emily enter the party arm in arm, whispering to each other and giggling. The rest of the family piles in behind them, with Grandma Winnie lingering in the lobby to greet the townsfolk.

Desirae slinks behind the group. Maddie thinks the child's black and grey outfit is more appropriate for a funeral than a Christmas party. Desirae hasn't worn the clunky boots since the episode with Grandma Winnie.

Maddie leans toward Emily, "Why did she even bother to come if she doesn't like it?"

"It's part of the protocol."

"Protocol?"

They check their coats with a young man in a red vest and continue into the main room, dimly lit, and decorated with wreaths and twinkling white lights. A towering, wide Christmas tree surrounded by wrapped gifts towers to the ceiling on one end of the room. On the other end, a band sets up.

"Yes," Emily continues, "it's like homework from her coach. She has to do things to learn to get out of her comfort zone and be more …social."

"Well, that makes sense. If she has anxiety or whatever, it's good for her to challenge herself to socialize."

Emily gives Maddie a patronizing look, "Oh, she's got something but it's not anxiety." Her eyes become piercing, her voice somber, "But she better get her act together. People around here don't tolerate *antisocial* behavior."

A slender man with a full beard and lively brown eyes rushes toward them. Maddie recognizes him as the town's librarian. He reaches out his arms, hands outstretched in a welcoming gesture. Maddie's met him before at work, but he doesn't seem to recognize her. He embraces Emily in a brief hug. "It's good to see you. Have you thought about volunteering at the library again? The kids loved your arts and crafts program."

"I didn't know you did arts and crafts at the library," Maddie began, wondering what, if anything, Emily can't do.

"I miss the kids! But you know, I've just been so busy planning the wedding."

"And I will be heartbroken for life if I'm not invited," he jokes.

"You and Becca are definitely invited. I'll be heartbroken for life if you don't come!" She turns to Maddie then, "Dan, have you met Maddie? She's the new sister my family *adopted*."

Emily exaggerates the word adopted and Maddie thinks it's a running joke. Maddie extends a hand to shake but is taken by surprise when Dan sweeps her into a hug.

"It's nice to meet an honorary Harris."

"Hey, actually, Maddie is an artist. She's a graphic designer, she may be a good person to do arts and crafts at the library, what do you think, Maddie?"

She hadn't thought about it. Maddie was never a kid person. But that was then. This is a new time and a new place. Perhaps, she thinks, in Silver Spring, Maddie is a kid person after all.

"Oh, sure. Sign me up."

Emily continues to mingle, introducing Maddie to the few townspeople she hasn't met yet. After cocktail hour winds down, they find the Harrises and Glen at a table near the front of the room.

"The party is catered by Mrs. Warren's restaurant, it's the one at the center of downtown, the Pine Grill. Best food in town, but don't tell the Mitchells, they own the pizzeria, which is good if you're in the mood for casual dining," Billie Jo informs Maddie.

One bite of the eggplant parmesan and Maddie knows she wasn't kidding. The band takes a break for dinner and a man Maddie recognizes as the mayor runs through a list of thanks before moving on to speeches.

Desirae, seated across from Maddie, mumbles in response to the mayor's comments. She doesn't have to be so annoying, Maddie thinks, even for an angsty teen. The mayor seems nice.

"And I want to thank everyone who contributed to our gift drive for the people of Greenridge," the room erupts in applause.

No one hears Desirae yell now, more than a grumble or a whisper, she stands up, facing the mayor, pointing an accusing finger, and shouts something Maddie doesn't understand. Something about

Greenridge. While the audience continues their applause, Mark and Grandma Winnie try to subdue Desirae. Maddie still can't tell what the girl is saying, but whatever it is, it's rude. She feels bad for the Harrises. Emily's face is red with embarrassment. Such a nice family, Maddie thinks, they don't deserve to be stuck with an unruly child. And her outburst is ruining the party.

Two men appear from the distance and grab both of Desirae's arms, walking her from the table. She tries to follow them with her gaze but just then, the mayor calls Grandma Winnie to the front to speak on behalf of the Preservation Society. Grandma Winnie stands and makes her way to the front of the room, ignoring the commotion.

Everyone ignores it. Maddie wants to see who the men are and where they are taking Desirae, but she subdues her curiosity not wanting to add to the scene. Maybe it's best they removed her before she could completely ruin the event.

Billie Jo and Mark don't seem worried. Maybe her family hired those men to do some kind of intervention if Desirae becomes too emotional.

She turns her attention to the front of the room again and listens to Grandma Winnie's speech.

"…and we know how fortunate we are to live in a place like Silver Spring. A place that is special because we are so careful about how we treat our community. And we know this is a luxury not everyone can enjoy. We know that we are unique. But we also recognize we have a duty to be charitable to those who are less fortunate."

Applause again.

She claps along with the crowd, beaming with pride to be a part of this generous family, for that's clearly how she sees herself now, as a Harris.

After the speeches and the dinner, a server brings pie and cookies for dessert. Desirae has not returned. Maddie thinks she may be in a time-out room somewhere, probably relieved to have found a way to blow off the party. She pities the girl but is also glad there will be no more disruptions.

"Maddie, I don't know if you noticed," Emily leans in confidentially, "but David Croft, over there, no, no don't look, don't look yet," she grabs Maddie's arm and leans in closer, "he has been seriously checking you out all night."

Maddie laughs.

"I can introduce you later?"

"I don't know," Maddie starts to say she isn't interested in a relationship. But why isn't she? Now that she's settled down maybe she is ready to date.

"Okay, now look, but quickly, don't stare."

Maddie pretends to sweep the room, looking in the direction Emily indicated. She recognizes David Croft. She's seen him in the town. His back to Maddie for the moment, he pushes blonde hair away from his eyes. He sips wine, full focus on an older man who gestures wildly as he tells a story or joke.

David is clean-shaven. With warm eyes. She can imagine him staring down at her.

"He's a teacher. History. I know what you're thinking, not a lot of money," Emily lowers her voice conspiratorially, "but you don't have to worry, his family is old money. He's not in something lucrative like development, teaching is a noble job," Emily picks a cookie apart as she gives this analysis.

Maddie snaps out of the fantasy.

I'm being silly. I don't even know him.

"There seems to be a lot of developers," she tries to change the subject, "but this town seems… I don't know, developed? I mean, what is there left to develop? Silver Spring is perfect."

"It is," Emily agrees, between bites of a cookie, "but the areas around here? They're atrocious. So, we need to help improve them. They've just become so… blighted. Really bad. But who better to fix that then the people who built this beautiful town, right?"

Maddie nods. She sees a shadow out of the corner of her eye. Focusing her gaze, she spots a piece of pie crust that has fallen to the floor. It slides once, then twice.

Maddie freezes, breath catching in her throat.

A rat tugs at the end of the dessert. The rat sees Maddie, holding her gaze for a moment, before gripping the remaining treat in his mouth and scurrying under the table next to hers.

Her stomach lurches, but she tries to forget. She doesn't want to make a scene, imagining the chaos that would ensue if anyone saw the vermin.

* * *

Maddie assumed Desirae would join them when the party was over. But she and Emily met Billie Jo, Grandma Winnie, Mark, and Glenn in the SUV and once she closed the car door, Billie Jo pulled away from the curb.

Maddie is stunned. She asks as delicately as she can, "Um, did Desirae leave already?"

"Desirae is with her coach, dear. She's going to be busy for a while, I'm afraid," Grandma Winnie's voice is distraught. Maddie sees a worried look on the older woman's face that hasn't been there before.

"Oh, was her coach there? I haven't met her yet." Maddie tries to sound upbeat.

"No, she hasn't had much time for socializing," Emily adds, re-signed, "I think Desirae is keeping her busy."

"Desirae better get with the program," Billie Jo sounds bitter, echoing Emily's earlier words. "She's doing far more damage than she can repair. Someday it will be too late."

Mark whispers something to Billy Jo that sounds like "Not now," but Maddie can't hear him, and it seems best to change the subject.

"David Croft was watching our Maddie, Mom," Emily teases.

"Well, that's not a bad match at all, is it, Grandma Winnie?"

Grandma Winnie looks into the distance, she says, "No, not at all," but her voice is absent.

"Speaking of Mr. Croft," Glen interjects, "I heard he has a new assistant, someone from out of town."

"Is that so?" Billie Jo asks, her voice flat.

Maddie understands this to mean he's taken. Her heart sinks, making her feel embarrassed for having such foolish ideas as romance with a man she's only seen once across a room.

She stares out the window at the night sky. Snow begins to fall on the drive home but makes no impact on their trip. She thinks again of Camelot. She had been the understudy for Jacqueline, but Jacqueline would never miss a performance. She had all the lines memorized anyway. And all the words to the songs, even if she didn't sing them.

She forgot since then, but it comes back to her bit by bit.

There was a legal limit to the snow…. And winter ends, March the second. She recalls Jake Marino, who played King Arthur, standing on the stage, singing in his baritone voice that made him the butt of jokes in elementary school but a heartthrob in high school.

"I know it sounds bizarre," he intoned, "but that's just the way things are."

He was wrong, she thinks, drifting to sleep to the road noises, the spot for happy-ever-aftering is Silver Spring.

CHAPTER 14

The library is as charming as Maddie expected. The exterior made of stone like a cottage in a fairy tale. Wood trim around the doors and windows, the two-story building stood on the corner of the main street, a row of shrubs lining the walkway to the entrance.

Accustomed to seeing rows of computers, DVDs, and three-dimensional printers at her local library, Maddie is charmed and surprised by the quaint interior. Emily holds her elbow gently and leads her to the back room where low tables are set with paper and markers.

Emily points to the cabinets where art supplies are kept. Children file into the room. They sit in the small chairs, keeping their heads down. One child, a boy with freckles and wide, curious eyes, points to Maddie.

"You didn't come from here," he announces.

Maddie feels her face grow hot, as if this child has just announced her deepest secrets. Emily walks toward the boy, leaning down to speak to him, but before she can, a woman rushes across the room, heels clicking on the floor.

"Jonathan," the woman's voice stern, causes the child to jump. The boy turns to look at her, eyes stunned.

"It's okay, I am new in town," Maddie offers, her heart softened by the fear in the boy's eyes.

"But mother," the boy begins, but his mother stands directly over him. He closes his mouth and looks down at the table.

"Did you forget your manners? Don't embarrass your family," she scolds.

"Yes, mother," he replies. His voice flat.

"Really, it's an innocent mistake," Maddie tries to intervene. The boy's mother's face is unreadable. Her tone curt.

"These behaviors must be dealt with early. We wouldn't want the boy to end up on the path to coaching. Or in Greenridge."

Before Maddie can ask any questions. Emily steps between Maddie and Jonathan's mother.

"It's so nice to see you again, how is Ben?"

The conversation drifts to small talk as Emily walks the woman to the door. The rest of the day is uneventful. Emily assigns a topic: Respecting Our Friends. The children draw pictures interpreting this theme.

When it's time for the children to reunite with their parents after about an hour, Maddie and Emily compliment them on their work. Of the dozen children assembled, Maddie notices almost all have drawn a ring of children in a circle. Variations on blobs with legs or more evolved stick figures in an arc cover most of the papers.

Jonathan's drawing is different.

She spots his drawing from several feet away. A stick figure wears a bow, along the bottom of the page, outlines of flowers sprawl up from the pointy green grass.

His mother clicks her tongue, "No trucks? I see." She turns and walks away.

CHAPTER 15

Maddie forgot the rat from the Christmas party, just like she forgot the rat crawling down the doll house in Emily's room during the first few days of her stay. But that changed on the day she saw the third rat.

* * *

By the morning of Arianna's wedding, Maddie no longer feels like an outsider. Wedding Fever, as Glenn jokingly refers to Emily's obsession with helping to plan every detail, has gotten to Maddie too. Arianna, a young woman with long, wavy hair the color of chestnuts and deep green eyes was more demure than Emily. In all their time together as a trio choosing gowns, picking the perfect wedding cake, and stuffing invitations into envelops, Maddie hardly knew anything about the woman. But nevertheless, Maddie spends the morning staring into the mirror making sure her hair and makeup were perfect, giddy about the celebration of romance later that day.

The weather, as always, is perfect. Cool, but sunny. Maddie loses track of time when the sound of a car pulling into the driveway pulls her from her preening. She gives her now almost ear-length hair one final pat, smoothing the fly-aways before running down the stairs.

The door bursts open and Emily rushes into the house with Glen trailing behind her. She doesn't seem to even notice Maddie at first.

"Mom? Mom! Are you ready? Is everybody ready? Grandma Winnie…" Emily calls up the stairs, picking up the skirts of her gown and climbing the steps two at a time.

Maddie leans against the threshold between the hallway and living room. She announces her presence before her friend is out of earshot. "Hi, Emily, nice to see you."

Her tone is light, she's amused at Emily's tunnel vision. Maddie heads toward the store, grabbing her jacket from a line of hooks on the wall.

Glen, who silently trailed through the door behind his future wife, stands in the corner. He shrugs, smiling at Maddie as if to say, 'What can you do? Wedding Fever.'

"Don't take it personally, she's been like this since yesterday. She hasn't even said good morning to me, yet."

"Well, it's a big day. She's the Maid of Honor in her best friend's wedding."

"You don't need to remind me. I can't wait until all this wedding stuff is over."

"All this wedding stuff? Aren't you excited? Only a few more months to go?"

"I'm excited, but all the women's stuff, the fussing and planning, is too much for me. I just leave her to the girls' stuff, and I write the checks," he laughs.

Maddie has gotten used to this type of sentiment. It used to surprise her, but now she shrugs it off. People in Silver Spring are old-fashioned. She doesn't want to argue with him over terminology. That's something her friends back home would have done, but she doesn't want to be that person. When in Rome, she thinks.

"I'm surprised Emily isn't splitting it with you. She's a modern woman."

Glen's face changes in an instant, giving Maddie the sickening feeling she said something she shouldn't have.

"No, ma'am, no wife of mine has to come out of pocket for her special day. Now, if she wants to open her purse when it's time to get our daughter horseback riding lessons? That's a different story."

He doesn't sound offended. But his change in tone surprises her. Emily's smart. She's confident. Why would she want a man to pay her way?

She catches a glimpse of motion from the corner of her eye and turns toward the stairs. Grandma Winnie, perfectly coiffed, walks toward them wearing a royal blue dress and pearls.

"Grandma Winnie, you look stunning. Will you save a dance for me?" Glen's face brightens as he welcomes the matriarch. She walks down the stairs gracefully despite some unsteadiness. She does look stunning, Maddie thinks.

I can only hope to age as well.

"I don't know, Glen, my dance card is already filling up, but I can put you on my waitlist." She puts a hand on each side of his face and pulls him toward her for a peck on both cheeks, leaving a hint of her trademark maroon lipstick.

He waits until she has turned her back before wiping the marks away with a handkerchief.

"Grandma Winnie, you look beautiful," Maddie adds. The older woman is radiant, she looks years younger, and it isn't the makeup.

"Thank you, dear," Grandma Winnie smiles, "I watched Arianna grow up beside my Emily. She's like my third granddaughter," her smile widens.

Billie Jo comes down the stairs next. She reminds Maddie of a mix between Jennifer Coolidge and Julie Roberts. Maddie envies Emily for inheriting her mother's beauty, feeling self-conscious. She pats her head and pulls at her hair, trying to tame its fuzzy nature.

She can't compete with women like Emily.

But she doesn't need to.

All eyes will be on Arianna.

"Okay, it's time to go it's time to," Emily rushes down the stairs, nearly tripping on her gown. "Where's Desirae?"

"Your father will drive her separate, don't you worry, just focus on Arianna's big day," Billie Jo reassures her.

On the way to the church, Grandma Winnie recounts stories from Emily's youth with the bride-to-be.

"They were good girls, but they were too clever. Got up to mischief, but nothing bad." The matriarch leans back, eyeing Emily from the passenger seat, and asks, "Do you remember when the two of you made up your minds you were going to marry the Sheridan brothers, even though they used to pull your hair and throw dirt at you?"

"Yes, Grandma Winnie," Emily's cheeks redden, she turns to Maddie, explaining, "we always dreamed about this day. And then in July, Arianna is going to be my Maid of Honor. We planned it all when we first became best friends in the second grade."

"I'm hardly part of the equation, just helping them fulfill their prophecy," Glenn wiggles his fingers on the word "prophecy" as if feigning a magic invocation. They laugh, but Emily begins biting her nails when they pull into the parking lot. The Cathedral of St. Benedict is a stone building with stained-glass windows imported from France. Maddie learned this detail at work. Each window is a scene portraying triumph of virtue over vices.

"Don't worry," Glen reassures Emily, You've waited since grade school for today, relax and enjoy it."

* * *

Emily and the rest of the wedding party were immediately ushered away, whisked from the crowd and into a back room to prepare. Maddie sits in the wooden pew with the Harris family and Glen.

Maddie runs the heel of her shoe against the wooden floor, smooth and shiny despite the repeated pressure of her foot. She's been inside a church three times. Once for a wedding, once for Christmas mass with her aunt's family, and once for her father's funeral.

She inhales, taking in the unique yet familiar scent. Churches always smelled the same. Like an open violin case. Not the violin itself, but the fragrance, an amalgamation of wood and strings, lingering inside the instrument's tomb.

Until now she forgot this universal church scent. Enduring regardless of celebration or mourning, Catholic or Episcopalian, they all share the same scent. Imprinted on her mind.

The white coffin, lined with flowers. A lone sunflower, sliding beneath the horizon of a wooden fence. A phone call in the middle of the night. Her mother, hysterical, on the kitchen floor, where Maddie found her pleading with God and banging her head against the wall as she sobbed louder than her baby cousin.

Someone's hand is on her shoulder now. She doesn't want more condolences, she wants…

"Maddie, honey," Grandma Winnie's voice brings her back.

She turns to see the older woman smiling down at her. Maddie's heart stops. Did she cry out loud? She blinks, her eyes are moist, but she doesn't feel tears on her face.

"I need to step out for a moment," she continues, then shields her mouth with a hand and whispers, "Restroom."

"Of course, I'm sorry, I was daydreaming."

Maddie stands so the older woman can walk past her.

She sits back down, turning to survey the room. The seats are filled, but Maddie is not surprised. It seems in Silver Spring, every event from baptisms to holiday celebrations to funerals is a reason for everyone to come together. Everyone is invited. Nobody gets left out.

Murmurs spread through the audience. The priest approaches the altar, then turns, and retreats to a back room. She thinks back to her musical theater days and imagines the priest retreating to the church's version of the green room. The place where priests go to wait for their cues.

"I think someone's late, probably the groom," Glen whispers.

Moments later, Grandma Winnie returns. Her eyes no longer bright with excitement. Her mouth turned down, lines on her face carved in worry. The older woman passes in front of her again, for the first time, Maddie thinks she looks her age. Maddie stands and whispers "Are you okay?" but Grandma Winnie doesn't hear her.

Time crawls.

The ambient conversation dies down until only murmurs and whispers remain. Maddie can hear the clock in the back of the room ticking softly.

It seems like a half hour, but that can't be right. The priest returns to the altar again. This time, he approaches the microphone. The crowd stands, and Maddie starts to get up as well. The priest raises his hands in a motion for everyone to return to their seats.

"I'm sorry, ladies and gentlemen. You may be seated. We have a slight delay it seems, but everything's fine. To help us out, Emily Harris has agreed to treat us to some of her delightful music."

As he says this, Emily emerges from the back room and approaches an organ in the corner. She looks terrified, Maddie thinks, wanting to hug her.

As if he can read her mind, Glen whispers, "It'll be good for her to play some songs."

Maddie nods. Despite Glen's attempt to sound reassuring. Maddie eyes his expression. He doesn't look convinced. His brow furrows and Maddie thinks he can read the anxiety pouring off his bride-to-be.

She watches Emily position herself at the organ. Her delicate hands hover above the keys for a moment. She leans toward the instrument and begins to play; sound fills the church. Maddie watches as her friend's fingers gracefully race across the keys. Maddie could play once, but that had been in the old house. Still, she could never play like Emily. Effortlessly, pulling notes from memory. Even from this distance, Maddie can see the worry on her friend's face. Another opening bar, she recognizes *Yesterday.* Maddie knows all the words to the song. She heard her mother sing it after imbibing enough to warm up her vocal cords when they lived in the tiny apartment in Poughkeepsie.

She scans the inside of the church. Floral arrangements line the aisle, altar, and each window. Their delicate petals look like silk. The arrangements are cream and lavender wrapped with braided purple and peach ribbons and traces of lace.

The audience claps as *Yesterday* ends. Without delay, Emily proceeds with the opening notes of an even older song, it's slow and she thinks it was originally by some guy named Melvin or Elvis or something. She's heard it before at anniversary parties and weddings.

She's lost in the melody when some of the lyrics come back to her mind.

"*Some things were meant to be....*"

And she can almost remember the name....

"*Take my whole life, too,*" she recalls a man singing.

Maddie feels something brush against her foot. She moves aside, not wanting to crowd Glen. She feels it again.

She looks at the floor in time to see a rat run past. Her breath catches in her throat. She mustn't react.

The melody echoes louder now. Beautiful and horrifying. From the corner of her eye she sees another rat, this one closer to the aisle. She snaps her head up, forcing herself to focus only on the altar. The piano, and the music.

Emily doesn't pause before beginning *Here, There, and Everywhere*, The song her aunt used to sing while rocking her baby cousin to sleep. One of many touchstones of warmth and attention she relished during school breaks when her mother couldn't get time off from work. The times her aunt would come to take her for the week.

The cherished breaks at her aunt's house were vacations from her life in Poughkeepsie. A reprieve from lurking in the shadows of her mother's grief and growing solace in bottle after bottle after new boyfriend. The vacations were never long enough and ceased altogether after a year, her aunt too consumed with parenting three children of her own, the youngest a toddler.

A heavy creak interrupts the memory. Around her, heads turn as the audience acts almost in unison, all parts of the same mass. The restless crowd shifts in their seats. She follows suit, turning in her chair, expecting to see Arianna in a veil and white gown adorned with tiny beads or lace. Even Emily hesitates for a moment. All eyes on the back of the room, whispers spread.

Two silhouettes appear in the threshold.

No luminous gown.

No lace veil.

She recognizes the asymmetrical haircut, the child's downcast eyes, and the stern look on the otherwise baby-faced older man.

Desirae and Mark enter the church and take their spots in the pew with the rest of the family.

The whispering stops. Emily picks up where she left off. Maddie wonders if this was the hold-up. But when the song finishes and Emily begins playing *Somewhere Over the Rainbow*, she knows realize this cant be true.

The crowd grows restless. People lean to each other and whisper, shifting in their seats as the song plays. No one chastises Desirae when she asks, louder than appropriate, "What the hell is going on?"

"I don't know," Maddie whispers to her, "The priest announced they're running late, I guess?"

Desirae scoffs, "If she had any sense she would run."

Maddie wants to ask what she means by that, but the priest returns to the altar. Emily finishes playing. Before she can start another song, the priest speaks.

"Everyone, everyone please, I'd like your attention." He's soft-spoken and it takes a moment for the crowd to quiet down and face forward. When the church is silent, he continues, "I'm afraid we are experiencing more of a delay than I thought, but I'm sure..."

He doesn't get the chance to tell the congregation what he is sure of. The doors open again, and everyone turns to face the back of the church. Maddie sees the tuxedo and assumes it is the groom. He takes two steps into the room and collapses, crying. A woman and several men seated in the back of the church rush to his side, trying to help him up, the crowd returns to whispering.

Maddie's heart freezes. She knows what is coming.

Hears the whir of the edger.

She knows if the groom weren't being held up by three men sur-rounding him, he would be on the floor. Wailing. Pleading with God. She knows by the contortion of his mouth, wide and stretched, the edges of his lips bent in an arch, his eyes, red, wet, and desperate, if he were not being restrained by the men, His body would find the floor. He would thrash himself against any nearby surface.

She even knows the sound it would make.

The sound of a head hitting a wall, repeatedly, a bass beat accentuating shrill sobs.

She knows the words before they come out of his mouth, open, and unable to hold back saliva.

The words that will spill forth once to the shock of all present before becoming a chant that he will recite as if in prayer.

"She's dead."

CHAPTER 16

It's only been three days, but Maddie's memory of the commotion has faded. She can barely picture Marcus- she heard someone call him that- burst into the church to announce Arianna's death. Since then, she's been walking through a fog.

Maddie sat absently through quiet dinners, the sound of silverware clinking against plates as the family, minus Emily, and Glen, quietly consume what is put before them.

The stillness unnerves her. Worse is Grandma Winnie's sudden timid appearance. Maddie doesn't know the matriarch's age, but since the wedding, or what should have been the wedding, the older woman looks burdened, exhausted, the weight of years of living etching crevices on her face, in her soul, that even the joys of a place like Silver Spring can't contain.

Last night, Billie Jo broke the silence.

"Arianna's memorial is tomorrow." Her voice cracks while speaking the deceased's name. She clears her throat, and continues, "Gonna be at the Hall."

Maddie understands that the Hall is the venue where the Christmas party had been held only a few months ago. She nods, cutting a piece of roasted chicken.

"Not the church?" Mark asks, wiping his mouth with a cloth napkin.

"No," Billie Jo answers, her voice flat. "Marcus's father suggested it. He's not doing well. Thought it would help him, to have different scenery."

Maddie notices Billie Jo flash a look at Grandma Winnie as she says this. She's relieved, whatever the reason, that they won't return to the church for the service.

Entering the hall at Arianna's memorial, Maddie replays the scene from dinner, wandering through the crowd at Ariana's memorial. Couples and families stand in clusters. Friends, neighbors, and colleagues embrace each other. She walks past them, a distant planet orbiting little galaxies. An occasional teary smile from a neighbor whose face she recognizes but name she doesn't, but no entry.

The Christmas decorations came down last month, and the hall is decorated for the upcoming Valentine's Day ball. Red and silver decorations cast an eerie glow in the dimly lit room. Maddie looks for a casket but sees none, only a guestbook, flowers, and a votive.

It must have been bad.

She recognizes the same flowers from Arianna's wedding, now on display to mark her eternal departure. She recalls a conversation she overheard between Grandma Winnie and Billie Jo last night.

"Florist went all out for the wedding. Not enough in stock for a memorial, so the family has decided to use the same arrangements," Grandma Winnie said.

"Tasteless." Billie Jo replied, a surprising note of disdain in her voice.

Grandma Winnie sighed and said something Maddie couldn't quite make out. It sounded like "She should've been the surrogate."

Maddie notices one of the arrangements has been damaged. The silk and lace torn, revealing a stem, slanted cut at the end, an open vein through which no blood flows.

It reminds her of the edger. She can hear it. Sees the sunflower drop. Cut down. Sliding out of her vision behind the white wooden fence. Only fifteen, but she understood. She feels her cheeks growing hot. But she mustn't cry like she had then. Not here. Not now.

She turns away from the flower, exposed for what all flowers are. Uprooted, mutilated, masquerading as pure. Her head spins. It can't happen here. She looks for something to hold on to. There are no tables set like the last time she was here. Only chairs, in rows, facing a microphone and projector screen on which a slideshow plays.

Gripping the back of a chair, she steadies herself. Deep breaths, the tingling in her head subsides. Maddie walks toward the slideshow.

She recognizes Arianna in photos that must have been recent. Another photo of two girls, about twelve. Emily smiles knowingly through the photo, standing arm in arm with her best friend. Her eyes twinkle as if she knows a secret, her grin devilish. Arianna looks mystified, innocent, as if she wasn't expecting to have her picture taken.

She looks around for Emily but doesn't see her amid the mourners. She recognizes David Croft and the librarian, Dan. She sees Mrs. Warren from the restaurant and even sees Janice, her boss. The Harris family mingles with their fellow townsfolk. A young woman talks with David briefly, her eyes nervous as she looks around the room. Maddie has seen her before. She always seems uptight, something unusual in Silver Spring. In fact, she looks uncomfortable, as if she wants to be anywhere but here.

I guess there's one in every town.

Maddie leaves the slide show, conscious of her status as an outsider. She wants to make space for those who knew Arianna. Wandering around the room, she notices Desirae in a corner, facing away from the crowd. The girl lifts a hand to her face and Maddie thinks she must be crying.

Maddie approaches, then hesitates. What if she says the wrong thing? What if Desirae goes into another tirade like at the Christmas party?

Better to ignore her.

Before she can retreat back into the crowd, Desirae turns and sees Maddie. The girl's bottom lip is quivering. Her face is streaked with tears.

Maddie takes a breath and approaches Desirae, halfheartedly extending an arm to hug. To her surprise, the girl wraps her in a tight embrace and cries on her shoulder.

The Child's sobs subside to sniffles and then clear. Desirae steps back, looking off to the side, avoiding eye contact with Maddie.

"I'm so sorry," Maddie offers, "I didn't realize you were close with Arianna. I mean, I should have known. She grew up with Emily. Must have been like family."

Desirae sniffles and laughs bitterly, shaking her head. "You have no idea. No one here does."

Oh, God, here we go.

"That's true. I don't know."

"Don't you think it was odd that she just happened to die the morning of her wedding?" Desirae asks in a conspiratorial tone.

"I mean, I guess. But, what happened? No one said how she died. Was it," Maddie hesitates and whispers, "an overdose?"

Desirae shakes her head instantly, wiping tears from her eyes, "No, no drugs aren't allowed in Silver Spring. Unless Dr. Needham hands them out," she says sarcastically, "and anyway Arianna wasn't into drugs. She was killed for another reason."

"Killed? What? How do you know?"

"I just know, okay? I know." She wipes her eyes again, stifling hiccups.

"Why would anyone kill her? Or anyone for that matter. Here, of all places, it just doesn't make sense…"

Desirae rolls her eyes, shaking her head as she laughs at Maddie's ignorance.

"She was going to call off the wedding."

"What? How do you know? So, you mean her fiancée, did it?"

"It's not that simple," Desirae begins. "Look around. There's no remains. No casket. Not even an urn."

"I noticed, but…"

"That's not a memorial. That's punishment. That's what happens when you…"

"Ladies, I'm so glad you're getting along, and Desirae, so nice of you to behave yourself."

Maddie jumps at first, even though she recognizes Mark's voice. She turns to see he has approached with Billie Jo. She doesn't know how long they were in earshot but Desirae clamps down and she doesn't want to sound silly by talking about this rumor of murder.

"Oh, yes, this is such a tragedy, I'm so sorry," she tells Mark. She doesn't mean to use cliches but can think of nothing else. She also knows it doesn't matter. She learned that almost fifteen years ago.

"It's like losing a daughter. I just can't believe it would come to this."

Billie Jo tightens her grip on his arm adding, "Who would expect, a funeral only days after the poor bird was due to be married."

"How is Emily?" Maddie asks. "I haven't seen her here."

"She's not well. Poor dear. They were like sisters. She hasn't come out of her room. I told her she should come pay her respects but, you know, grief happens in so many different ways."

Maddie nods.

Before the conversation can go any further, the priest calls everyone to take seats so the service can begin.

He speaks the prayers interspersed with memories of Arianna's life in Silver Spring, Maddie turns Desirae's words over in her mind. The kid is messed up. But would she really make up stories like that? About something so serious. And what did Mark mean when he said he couldn't believe it would come to this?

Screams erupt behind her, and Maddie turns toward the commotion. She sees row upon row of mourners jump to their feet, facing the ground and shrieking. She looks down as rats- at least a dozen- scamper across the floor.

CHAPTER 17

Gabriella

Gabriella is alone in the library's basement. It's the only place in Silver Spring she feels comfortable, mostly because no one bothers to come down here. Why would they? They don't want to know their history. They prefer the founding myths. No one takes the time examine the documents the townspeople have deemed worthy of preserving. And why store them for posterity, only to leave them buried in a dusty library basement?

Gabriella knows more about them than they know about her. But it's always that way with white people. She flips wavy brown hair over her. She's been here less than a year. More than a few months. Somehow, it's become harder to keep track with every passing day.

But however long it's been, she hasn't been able to overcome the feeling of being a stranger. She's used to the looks people give her as they encounter her walking down the street or in the stores. It's no different than most small, homogenously white towns. Which is why she usually avoids such places.

And how she came to be here? She can't say. Why would believe her? But she knows it wasn't exactly by choice.

She thought the presence of the new girl, or the new-new girl, would be a relief. Finally, the town would have someone else to adapt to. Watching the town embrace Maddie while still regarding her with suspicion was a painful reminder of something she shouldn't have let herself forget.

She could be here a decade, it wouldn't matter.

She turns another page in an old school yearbook from 1978. She doesn't know what she's looking for as she combs through the town's history. But something inside her is restless to dig while she's here.

Which can't be too much longer.

She tries not to think about home. By now she's probably lost her apartment, her belongings long since thrown to the curb for someone else to draw from. She knows she has no job to return to now. And if she and Brenda were still together at least someone would have tried to find her. Or reported her missing when she got lost. But she was out of Gabriella's life before she ended up here.

Losing her over something so stupid as a misunderstanding through text was bad enough. But then Gabriella had gone and gotten herself lost in a Sundown Town.

She knew it immediately. No sign necessary. She recognized the reactions in the body language from the townspeople. She recalls the first time she noticed this. In middle school when she was invited to Jennifer's pool party. Little did she realize at the time that if she, who spent more time in the library and staying after school to help teachers clean the chalkboards than going to girl scouts or joining clubs, had been invited to a party it was because everyone was invited.

Whether they were welcome or not.

Gabriella recalls watching from the passenger seat as her mother's face fell the closer they got to Jennifer's house. The car slowed to a stop, her mother put a hand on her shoulder and said, solemnly, "Look, if you have any problems, anything at all, you don't feel good, you want to come home? Ask to use their phone and call me, okay?"

She was too busy smiling and imaging swimming with the other kids to understand her mother's words. But she learned soon enough.

At school, almost everyone got called names. It was like each kid had their season. The chubby kids, the kids with glasses, the kids who were too smart or not smart enough, but there were enough people to cycle in and out of the bullies' attention that the bullying never lasted too long. She wasn't naive. She knew that there were certain words reserved only for her and her cousins but not the other kids.

But this was different, she thought, leaving the car, and waving goodbye to her mother, swimsuit in a bag over her shoulder. This was a party. And she was invited.

Jennifer's house was a mansion compared to any houses in her neighborhood. Before she even climbed the front steps, a neighbor, an older woman, rushed in her direction, waving a newspaper at her as if she was a dog who just peed on the floor.

"Are you lost, miss?"

She blushed, "No, I'm here for the party."

The old woman didn't seem to believe her, but before she could object Jennifer's mother was at the door, waving her inside. Things went downhill from there. That was the day Gabriella learned that bullies weren't always obvious. Sometimes they ignore you. Or question everything you say. Or ask aloud in a crowded room how you could afford to buy the swimsuit you had on.

Since then she dreaded visiting places like that neighborhood. Until she had the misfortune of becoming lost in a fog and ending up in an entire town of Jennys and old women who would shoo at little girls with newspapers.

A click from the hallway and the lights growing dim is Gabriella's cue that the library is closing. No one bothered to tell her directly. The only one here who speaks to her much is David. Others are polite but avoid her. They eye her with a mixture of curiosity and suspicion. They've even given her a new name: Gabrielle.

CHAPTER 18

March 2023

Maddie

In the weeks following Arianna's memorial, Maddie runs arts and crafts at the library alone. In the Harris household, two empty chairs mark Emily and Glen's continued absence from the dinner table. The first week, dinners were somber. Even Desirae was subdued.

Maddie waited for news of Emily, but to her surprise, no one in the household spoke about her. No mention of her name, or discussion of how she was faring. Billie Jo didn't call to talk to her on the phone, or at least not when Maddie was around.

One night after dinner, Maddie approaches Billie Jo. The older woman retired from the table early and sits on an upholstered chair in the corner of the living room. She looks through a book, the corners rough and worn.

She notices Maddie approach and sets the book down, covering it with her hands and regarding Maddie with a thin smile.

"I was thinking," Maddie begins, she avoids looking Billie Jo in the eye and instead studies a knot in the wooden table beside her. "Maybe it would be good to stop by and see Emily. If you think she's ready for company?"

Billie Jo's face brightens, but Maddie can see the fatigue in her eyes. She's never looked so tired.

"That's a great idea. She hasn't had much to say to me, but you know how it is," Billie Jo looks weary, Maddie also thinks she looks close to tears. "You know, I'm mom, but you are her friend, you're closer in age, she may open up to you."

Maddie doesn't want to correct Billie Jo's assumption. There's at least a seven-year difference in their ages.

"That's great," she replies, "I can Google her address and…" she remembers, again, she doesn't have her phone. Billie Jo looks confused, but then recovers her haggard demeanor.

"I can drop you off on the way to take Desirae to her coach, it's no trouble. And then you'll know the route and can visit whenever you'd like."

***

Maddie drifted to sleep early that evening. When she wakes, it's full dark. She pulls herself up and slinks to the bathroom to brush her teeth, eyes still bleary with sleep.

Voices drift from behind a closed door. She stops, rubs her eyes, and listens. She shouldn't. It's rude. Whatever is being said in private behind Billie Jo and Mark's bedroom door is not meant for her ears. But she can't resist. Especially when she hears Arianna's name.

Adrenaline surges and Maddie is awake now. She recognizes Grandma Winnie's voice, but her words are muffled. Something about Arianna. She hears the words "Fall Bride," and turns her head to the side, wondering if Arianna hadn't wanted to cancel her wedding after all. Had she only wanted to delay until fall? Had someone killed her for that? And what will the townspeople do?

The voices continue in hushed tones, she can no longer hear what they say. Maddie continues to the bathroom. She brushes her teeth, staring at her disheveled short hair in the mirror, her eyes bloodshot. In other places, a tragedy like this would be the talk of the town. She thinks of the reactionary response to school shootings and abductions, other acts of violence. But in Silver Spring, there had been no statement from the mayor. No constant news cycle, not even a call for people to lock their doors. She spits toothpaste into the sink and runs the water, filling her glass to swish and spit again.

It's all nonsense, she thinks. Whatever happened to Arianna, it wasn't murder. Desirae is mistaken, and she is being silly taking cues from a moody, petulant child.

Emily and Glen live in a cottage-style home. Like most of the houses in Silver Spring, it's two stories high. The home has a pale yellow exterior. The lawn is immaculate. Ivy climbs around a stark white columns on both sides of the front steps. Maddie knocks on the lavender door. Moments later, Glen answers. He smiles and waves to Billie Jo and Desirae. They pause for a moment to wave back before driving away.

"Thanks for coming," Glen's voice is sincere but shaky. Dark circles hang beneath his eyes. Maddie can see the worry in his expression.

He closes the door behind her. The house smells like roses. Maddie notices Glen isn't wearing shoes and slips out of her sneakers. The carpet is soft, almost buoyant. She wonders if it is newer and less tread upon than the one in her parents' home.

Maddie follows Glen into the living room and then stops.

She expects Emily to be depressed but she isn't prepared for the sight of her friend, legs tucked under an oversized sweatshirt, diminutive and frail, face sunken, purple, puffy skin holding up her bloodshot eyes.

"I should warn you," Glen whispers too late, "she isn't doing well," he says this in front of his fiancée as if she isn't there. She shows no signs of hearing.

Glen's eyes are bloodshot. Far from his normally youthful face, his eyes are circled in shadows. He seems to have aged a decade since she saw him last.

Maddie nods and sits in the armchair beside Emily. The younger woman stares into space. Maddie wonders if she saw her. She reaches a hand to her friend, resting it on her hand, then hesitates and pulls back. Emily's body has become angular. Maddie realizes the sweatshirt isn't one of Glen's. It's one she's seen Emily wear before, but back then it fit snugly. Now, Emily is drowning in it.

The vacant look on Emily's face, the way she has retreated into a small corner of the chair is familiar. Maddie saw her mother slip down the same spiral after her father was killed in the hit-and-run accident. She wonders if Emily is only in the chair on her account. Her mother's grief kept her resigned to a corner of a guest bedroom for days at a time. She chain-smoked and even sent Maddie to the store with a note to get more cigarettes and alcohol when everything in the family's liquor cabinet was gone.

Her mother wilted away for months. By the time she found roots again, it was too late. Emily may not be there yet but doesn't have far to go.

"Emily, honey, I'm so sorry." Maddie stops, not sure what to say next.

Emily blinks, she starts to smile but pauses halfway, "Thanks, I'm sorry. I haven't been in the mood to leave the house." Her voice is barely above a whisper.

"I do understand. I mean, I don't know what it's like to be you, and I didn't know Arianna," she chooses her words carefully, not wanting to open doors if she's not prepared to venture across the threshold, "but I know what it's like to lose someone close, and I'm here for you."

Emily starts to slide, her hair spilling over the back of the chair. She reaches her legs out from beneath the sweatshirt, steadying herself with her feet.

A stabbing feeling in her heart makes Maddie suddenly want to cry. She closes her eyes tight, and opens them, trying to focus only on this moment.

"Can I get you ladies anything to drink?" Glen asks, leaning over Emily, putting a hand on her shoulder and kissing her head.

"No, I'm okay," Emily shakes her head.

"Same here, thanks though," Maddie replies.

Glen nods and looks around awkwardly before leaving the room. Now it's just her and Emily. She doesn't know what to say.

"I don't know what I can do, Emily, but I'm here for you if you need anything." She knows words are insufficient. For what seems like an hour, they sit together in silence.

"Do you want to go for a walk?" the younger woman asks, startling Maddie, who had begun drifting into daydreams.

"Sure, yes, anything you want."

They leave the house. Emily has gotten so small Maddie worries she'll freeze or collapse. But she takes a deep breath, and, in the sunlight, Maddie thinks her friend looks better already. Maddie turns in the direction of the town but realizes Emily has begun walking the other way. She corrects herself.

"I've never gone in this direction, this will be nice," she comments.

"Yes, it's different. But I don't have the energy to run into people in town and deal with the looks and the conversations and," Emily catches Maddie's eyes and quickly adds, "oh, not you, it's different with you. I mean like, you know, colleagues, acquaintances, nosy neighbors and all."

Maddie understands.

"What's down this road?" Maddie asks, eager to change the subject now that an opportunity has presented itself.

"Well, it's residential for another mile or two, but the neighborhoods here are older as you get farther away. If you keep going eventually you get to Greenridge. But that's far to walk and besides no one from Silver Spring has any reason to want to go there."

Maddie nods. She can see no reason anyone from Silver Spring would want to go anywhere but here.

They walk in silence. The air is pleasant for early spring. Not warm but comfortable with a jacket. It's sunny finally, and the snow has mostly melted leaving reminders that lawns will soon re-emerge.

Maddie is entranced by the rhythm of their footsteps set against, the singing of daring birds beginning work early, and the occasional passing car. They walk with only ambient noise as the backdrop. The serenity is broken after what seems like an hour when Emily speaks, her voice now stronger.

"What do you really think of Silver Spring?" she asks.

Maddie stops walking, surprised by the question.

"I love it, why? Does someone think I don't?"

Emily has also stopped walking. Hands in her pockets, she shifts from side to side, looking into the air as if searching for what to say next.

"It's not that. But, it's just that you're from somewhere else. And I've never been anywhere else. I was just wondering what someone from away thinks of our town."

Maddie shrugs, "It's perfect. Don't you think? I mean, I've never seen anyplace like it. The people are all friendly. Even Desirae, who's a little bit of a lot, even she's got a good heart when you really talk to her, but you know that."

Emily nods slowly. In the silence that follows Maddie considers telling Emily about her conversation with Desirae the day of the memorial but decides against it. She doesn't want to open that can of worms unnecessarily.

"So, you've really never gone anywhere else? Like not even on vacation?"

Emily shakes her head. "My family is so steeped in the history of the town, it's like we can't leave. Not even for a weekend. We've always got a meeting with this committee or that auxiliary and I sometimes wonder if my mom thinks the town would collapse if she wasn't here." Maddie knows it's a joke, but she sees something sinister pass over her friend's face when she says this.

"But couldn't they just Zoom for their meetings?"

"Hmm?" Emily looks confused.

Maddie's eyes widen but she doesn't want to embarrass her friend.

"It's like an internet platform that lets you have meetings online. You know, the thing everyone used during the pandemic?"

Emily doesn't reply and instead makes the face Maddie has come to understand means 'I don't know what you're talking about, and I don't want to know, so I'll just change the subject.'

But now she's intrigued. "Didn't you shut down during the pandemic? Back in 2020?"

Emily looks uncomfortable but Maddie can't let this go. She knows some communities were defiant and wouldn't be surprised if she learned Silver Spring was full of anti-vaxxers, but the blank look on Emily's face at the mention of the pandemic is alarming.

"Silver Spring is different. It's not like other places. We don't have a lot of the… problems… other places have."

"Yeah, I guess," Maddie accepts her friend is going to remain closed-lipped on the topic of Covid. Is it possible they had no cases? She thinks she may never know.

"It's mostly good. But there are some things that I wonder. I wonder sometimes if some things are better in other places. Like… did you ever do something because it seemed like the best possible thing for everyone, like nothing could go wrong, but then there are consequences you don't think of until it's too late?"

Maddie's heart races.

You have no idea.

Maybe Emily does understand more than she lets on.

"Yes, you mean like you do something thinking it's right but then it's not and you regret it? Yes, I understand that."

Emily is silent for a moment. She runs a finger along the bark of a tree, looking troubled. Like she wants to say something but isn't sure if she should.

"Why don't you take a trip somewhere? With Glen? It might be good for you, you know?"

"We haven't had time. So much to do. Wedding preparation, you know?"

Maddie feels a sinking in her stomach. Poor Emily. The enormity of her friend's grief starts to set in. The constant reminders in this small town to say nothing of her upcoming wedding.

"Can you postpone the wedding?"

"No, that isn't an option. And I've fallen behind in preparations."

"Who can think about weddings at a time like this?"

She shakes her head. "I have to. It's the right thing to do. It's for everybody. For the town. We need something happy to celebrate. It's what Arianna would have wanted." She sniffs and wipes a tear away.

"I'll be happy to help with anything you need, as long as you're sure you want to do this."

"Thank you." Emily's eyes meet hers. "I appreciate you so much, Maddie. I know I haven't been a good friend, hiding away and sulking and all."

"You're fine. When you need space, it's okay. And when you need me to be there for you, I'm here for you. Whatever you need."

Emily inhales deeply, her expression lighter, less worried. Some of the sparkle returned to her eyes.

"Would you like to be my Maid of Honor, Maddie?"

Maddie's heart stops. Emily must have closer friends, women she's known since childhood? But what she says is, "Oh, my God, Emily, of course. If you're sure that's what you want?"

Emily nods.

"Yes, it's the best thing for everyone." She looks into the distance and then catches herself and adds, "It would mean the world to me."

Emily hugs her and Maddie gently wraps her friend in a soft hug, afraid still of how small she's gotten. Still enwrapped in a hug, Maddie asks, "Will you try to do something for me?"

"Sure," Emily agrees, still holding tightly.

"Will you try to play piano? And get your strength back?"

Emily hugs Maddie tighter and sobs. "Yes."

"And when you're caught up with planning, let's take a day trip, somewhere not too far. Maybe Lake Placid?"

Emily laughs through her tears. She pulls away and Maddie can see her eyes are alight. "I've always wanted to go there. Yes. Maybe in a few weeks?"

The sun is high as they walk back to Emily and Glen's house. It's unseasonably warm. Emily talks about wedding plans, to Maddie's surprise. It seems to uplift her, so she lets her chatter on about types of buttercream cakes and the bands they have to audition.

They're a block shy of their destination when someone calls out from across the street.

"Emily!"

They look up in time to see David Croft walking briskly in their direction, a young woman behind him. Maddie recognizes her from the Christmas party and Arianna's wedding. She's noticed the young woman is often on the outskirts of community events, but she doesn't know why. She's never been formally introduced.

"Hi, David, what a surprise seeing you here."

Emily's tone is polite, Maddie can't tell if she is being sincere.

"Well, I've been giving Gabrielle a tour. She's a newcomer who has been helping me with some research."

Something about the way he says "newcomer" makes Maddie flinch. Gabrielle has been here for at least as long as Maddie, and she doesn't feel like a newcomer. Is that how others refer to her behind her back? How they think of her? Her eyes sting with tears, but she blinks them away.

The young woman at his side smiles and waves nervously. She's petite and her dark hair spills in waves down her back. Maddie self-consciously reaches for her own hair, growing in wavy strands that always cling together in a tousled mess despite being combed throughout the day.

"Oh, well, that's great that you have someone new learning about our town's amazing history," Emily holds David's eyes locked in a stare as she says this.

"Speaking of people who are new to town," David eyes Maddie as he says this.

"Of course, I'm sorry, David, this is Maddie, she works at the Preservation Council now. She's a graphic designer."

"Nice to meet you both," Maddie adds.

"Oh, wow, design, hmmm, maybe we can collaborate on a presentation for the town?" David asks.

"Sure," Maddie shrugs. She avoids looking him in the eyes, certain she is blushing over their imaginary romance that lasted all of five minutes and existed only in Emily's and her imaginations.

"Great. Well, I won't hold you both up, I know you've had a lot going on, and," he looks at Emily as if he wants to say more, but his eyes dart in Gabrielle's direction and he only says, "We'll talk again, when it's, um, better timing."

When they are out of earshot Emily admits, "That wasn't so bad. But he's not nosy."

"Strange, right? I mean for a history teacher you would expect him to ask a lot of questions."

Emily finds this funny, and as with so many of the inside jokes in Silver Spring Maddie laughs along with her, uncertain as to why.

CHAPTER 19

Maddie's boss, Janice, sits beside her at the Silver Spring Town Council meeting. Maddie is already bored but she can't leave, not when Janice specifically asked her to come.

"Should I prepare a presentation?" Maddie asked.

"Yes. Maybe something like a Power Point? If that's not too much?"

It struck Maddie how technologically stunted Silver Spring is even in the twenty-first century. To Janice, this technology is a big deal like a flying car or teleporting.

"Oh, sure, I can put something together." Maddie has learned not to say things like 'Of course, a five-year-old can do that!' so as not to offend the traditionalists and technophobes at work.

A crowd files into Town Hall, Maddie's mind drifts to the awkward conversation that followed. She had scrolled through the archive of recent city events looking for images to use for the presentation, when something had occurred to her. She recalls knocking on Janice's door, gently bringing up her concern.

"We don't have a lot of diversity. In the photos."

Maddie had waited for a reply, but Janice stared at her as if she didn't understand.

"It seems like there are a lot of… um… *similarities*. In the photos of people in the last few years?" She hadn't meant to end on an upward lilt making her statement into a question.

"I don't know what you mean. We have over three hundred photos in the archive since last year," Janice began scanning through a file on her computer, an older model with a chunky monitor.

"Oh, yes, I looked through them, what I mean to say is," Maddie paused, "I mean, it's often attractive, like, it's a selling point, to be able to show that a community such as Silver Spring… has… um… diversity."

Janice looked up from the computer, eyebrows furrowed. "I don't follow you."

Maddie cleared her throat and tried a different approach, "What I mean to say is I don't have any photos that show how… um… like … they're nice pictures but it's a little… monochromatic?"

Janice nodded and Maddie thought she understood, but what she said next proved otherwise. "You mean we don't have a lot of… what do artists call it? Like undertones? In the pictures? Not enough contrast."

Maddie suddenly felt insufficient to finish the conversation she started. For the first time in months, she thought of Carolyn. Carolyn would be able to explain it, even if she would do it in that way she has of ruining everything for everyone.

"Contrast, yes, that's part of it, but also…" she struggled for the right words, "I think if we had more photos of Silver Spring's Black families? Or different ethnicities? To add to the slideshow, it would do a better job of showing how welcoming the town is."

Janice looked more confused than ever, sitting back in her chair then, "Didn't you feel welcomed in Silver Spring?"

"Oh, of course, yes," she hurried to correct herself.

"Well, that's a good idea, why don't you come with me and say a few words about how welcomed you felt here?"

"Um, I…" Maddie never spoke at a political meeting. Her stomach tightened. She wanted to refuse the offer but couldn't find a justification before Janice continued.

"I'll have Melissa write up a little script for you to follow, that way you don't have to feel nervous. Don't worry, you'll be great." Janice's face filled with the excitement of someone who just had a million-dollar idea. "I'm so glad you brought this to my attention. That's why we love fresh blood at Silver Spring, keeps the ideas flowing, you know?"

Since then, Maddie didn't bother reprising the conversation. She wanted to ask Emily about it, but her friend kept to herself a lot more since Arianna's death.

Janice interrupts her thoughts, "They are going to have some town business to discuss, and there is time set aside for public commentary, so we have some time before giving our presentation," she explains.

This news staves off some of Maddie's anxiety, but the thought of sitting through dry town business gives way to an urge to run from the room. She can't. She wouldn't. But she wants to.

The mayor calls the meeting to order. Maddie looks down at her lap for the first time in months expecting to see a phone. It dawns on her again her phone is gone. Her car is still in the shop. Ice crawls down her spine as she remembers the bizarre circumstances that brought her here. She can't believe she forgot. It was a kind of forgetting, wasn't it? To know something happened but relegate it to the salt marshes of your mind, losing all sight of it until a random impulse leads to recall?

That is, she thinks, the definition of forgetting.

I'll mention the car to Billie Jo again, she thinks. Part of her knows it doesn't matter. She has no place to go and if she did, why leave all this? A job, new friends, and a picture-perfect place. But it will be nice just to have it back. The bill for repairs if it's taken this long will be another story. She pushes the creeping feeling of worry down, burying it along with remnants of a life she forgot she had in the first place.

"We need to address," a man wearing khaki pants and a plaid sweater leans toward the microphone speaking to the council, "the dangerous outside influences disrupting this town. Threatening our way of life."

Maddie leans forward. He looks like he spent the day golfing. Thin wire glasses are perched at the end of his nose. His face is round, and it looks as if he's growing out a beard or trying to. He continues, "Whoever killed Arianna…"

Maddie is alert now. Did he say killed? That's what Desirae implied. Come to think of it, there had been no follow-up. She hadn't heard any mention of Arianna's death from anyone. Nothing until now.

The man continues, "Precious Arianna, this town's virgin bride, full of promise…" He removes his glasses and gestures as if wiping his eyes.

Maddie grimaces, still shocked, now offended, did he say virgin? She wants to ask Janice how he could possibly know whether Arianna was a virgin and who cares anyway when you're dealing with murder, but she remains silent.

"And of course, I don't believe it's a coincidence that both the murder and the surge in the rat population have come at the same time that people from away…" he side-eyes Maddie, then turns his head to glance across the room. Maddie follows his gaze and recognizes David Croft. Not David, she realizes, he's looking at a girl seated next to him. Maddie realizes this must be his new assistant.

"But the real threat, the real danger, is that we've been too lenient with those people at Greenridge."

Those people, huh? You picked some winners, girl. Maddie hears Carolyn's voice.

The man continues, "We all understand there was a time when we needed them, we had a mutually beneficial arrangement. But, thanks to our fortunate circumstances in recent years, this is no longer the case…"

"Sir," the mayor stands, holding up a hand to cut the man off, "I hear your comment and there is no need, I mean to say you've reached your time limit, sir, so thank you for your comment."

Maddie wants to ask what he's talking about, but the next speaker has already approached the microphone.

"June Warren, lifelong resident of Silver Spring, and while I don't love the prior gentleman's lack of discretion, I want to echo some of his sentiment," she begins. Her tone is like a sweet aunt. Nonthreatening. Sensible. She continues, "our restaurant has been impacted by the, um, rat situation, okay? This has never happened before. It is not a reflection of our business. It is a change in the town. And now our business is in danger, not to mention health issues. And we all care about safety, right?" she pauses for impact.

"Now, as for the touchy subject of the Greenridge people, I have to agree, council. We've been more than generous with them. But they take advantage of our kindness. They beg, sir. Outside our business? And it's unsightly. It's bad for business. They are unclean, they don't shower, they don't hold the same values we have here and that's fine, but they shouldn't be able to come to our town if they don't respect what we value, sir, and that's all I wanted to say."

The next three commenters echo this sentiment. Maddie thinks Greenridge sounds familiar, but it takes a woman who identified herself as a stay-at-home mom and of course, a lifelong resident, to help her connect the dots.

The Christmas party. All those gifts wrapped in shiny paper and elaborate bows under the gigantic tree had been for the people of Greenridge. All donations. Well, that was nice, Maddie thinks.

But who are the people of Greenridge? She jogs her memory but can't recall seeing anyone begging outside of any stores. There was the woman in the orange dress and the crown of leaves, but every time she brought up this vision, people acted like they hadn't seen her, so they couldn't be bothered by the person Maddie had assumed was an apparition.

By the fifth comment, Maddie is becoming bored with the monotony of opinions. It seems if there is a problem that poor people are breaking the rules, the police will deal with them and that's all. No need to go on and on about it.

"I'm not going to be PC about this," a man in a suit approaches the microphone next. "We are talking about squatters. Illegal squatters in Greenridge. And all our charity, though it was well-intentioned, it was clearly a mistake…"

Maddie's heart sinks. She feels panic coated with bile rising. She understands now. Her breathing quickens, but it's all shallow. In her chest. She can't slow it down.

"And the fact is, they can work. I've even offered many of them jobs. They show up drunk if they show up at all and some of them turn me down because they can make more money begging."

Maddie's head spins. She's heard this before.

She wants to stand up and scream. To tell them it's not like that. Not that simple. Images flash in her mind. Morning frost on her windshield in the Walmart parking lot. A mother and child getting out of their car ahead of her. The child raising her arms to the sky, her mother lifting her, then running to the store for a reprieve from the elements. Families walking back to their encampments, hurrying past hecklers who throw rocks at them. The man with white hair knocking on her car window.

"And so, we just need to drive them out. Get them off the street. Lock them up if they don't want to follow the law and work like the rest of us."

Her heart races. His words are met with applause. Not just applause, a standing ovation. Janice looks down at her, arching her brow in surprise.

Maddie grips the seat of her chair; she wills herself to stand but can't. The applause continues. *Mustn't draw attention.* She's the only one seated. Janice still watching. She forces herself to her feet. Closes her eyes to hide tears. Even in the darkness, the room spins. Her chest hurts. She's having a heart attack. Her head is light and fuzzy for a moment when she collapses to the floor.

CHAPTER 20

Maddie is nauseous. The bright light above her doesn't help. This time she doesn't wonder where she is. She doesn't wake as Madison but Maddie. Which is why she hears so many people murmuring her name.

"She's okay, she's okay," she hears a man reassure the crowd. Of course, she remembers, because she's at the town council meeting. Where she had a panic attack. Or passed out. Or did some such embarrassing thing in front of the entire town including her boss and now everyone will know she isn't Maddie. She's Madison, from the Hudson Valley, where she couldn't keep a job or an apartment and ended up living in her car in retail store parking lots.

"Please, let's give the young lady some space," the man continues. She recognizes him now. From this angle, his face reminds her of a gopher. A bespectacled gopher who stepped out of an L.L. Bean catalog. Maddie feels sick as she realizes that the man sitting over her, hand on her wrist taking her pulse, looking down at her with bulging eyes is the same man who moments ago called on the town to lock up the people from Greenridge.

People like her.

"Miss, it's okay, you just had some anxiety. It's okay," he continues.

"Oh, Dr. Needham it's a good thing you were here tonight," Janice adds. Maddie sees her boss leaning over the doctor's shoulder, eyes wide and fearful.

"She just had a little anxiety it appears," the doctor reassures Janice. "Not from around here, must have come as a shock to know there are still some bad elements in Silver Spring."

The doctor looks back down at Maddie and puts a hand on her shoulder in what was supposed to be an encouraging gesture. "Don't you worry, you're safe as can be at the Harris's home."

CHAPTER 21

Gabriella

Gabriella slips through the door, pulling her satchel out of the way and looking over her shoulder one last time to ensure no one has followed her.

You're paranoid, she tells herself

She wants to believe it. Wants to believe the smiles are sincere. But she can't. She locks the door behind her.

No one in Silver Spring locks the doors, David told her, when she first started interning with him.

But this, like many of the town's traditions, was something she couldn't adopt, even when she tried. She drops her satchel to the floor and retrieves a binder from the archives. Her heart races. If anyone finds out she removed it, there will be trouble. She doesn't know what, exactly. Stashing it in a dusty file cabinet in the corner of the cluttered room, she imagines herself defending her decision.

"I didn't realize it was still in my bag until I got home," she would say.

"Why would it be in your bag in the first place?" her interrogator would ask.

She shakes her head.

Have to think of something better.

Or you can just not get caught, she reminds herself.

It was hard enough getting through the town council meeting last evening without blurting out what was on her mind. But she had been surrounded. Even now, in the dimly lit room, the memory makes her shiver. One by one, they spoke about Greenridge with such hatred.

She recognized the narrative. The rhetoric painfully familiar. Yet as she searched the crowded meeting room, she only saw vengeance in their eyes. A strange bloodlust.

But then, she recalls, the evening ended in commotion. The new woman, Maddie, fainted clear away. What was that all about?

Typical pearl clutching? Shock spurred on by the talk of hordes of undesirables infiltrating the picture perfect town?

Or something else?

She thought she saw something pass over the woman's face even when she resumed consciousness. But Gabriella was careful not to get too close. Let the white people hover over the damsel in distress. She kept her distance, watching from the back of the room.

Still, she thought Maddie looked stunned, bewildered. Maybe the discussion triggered something for her.

Gabriella rubs her hands together, trying to keep warm in the cold room. Her mind drifts from the memory of the complaints about outsiders to a more distant memory. She and Brenda, huddled among a group from their Border Justice chapter. It was 2018 and they were among a dozen or so people gathered outside of their city hall to protest ICE raids on local restaurants where undocumented people had been employed. When they arrived, Gabriella's passion and intensity kept her adrenaline high. But her confidence faded at the sight of counter protesters. After an hour, they had been surrounded. Jeering from a crowd- some older but many young, in their twenties- escalated. They began throwing rocks, then bottles.

"Get down," Brenda tried to push her to the ground. She thought she was helping. But there were elderly people in their group. People who needed shielding much more than her. She broke from Brenda's grasp and tried to block an elder with her body but was too late. A bottle hit the woman's forehead, knocking her to the ground. A hospital visit and a dozen stitches later, and she was on the mend.

But Gabriella had nightmares for months about being surrounded.
In her dreams, she could see the rage in the eyes of strangers.
    And last night, she saw it again in real life.

CHAPTER 22

Maddie

Maddie is relieved to see Emily and Glen arrive for dinner a few nights later. From the cautious, watchful glances between Grandma Winnie and Billie Jo, Maddie can tell she isn't the only one worried about Emily. Only Desirae still looks as sullen as ever. And something is different about Grandma Winnie, but Maddie can't place what has changed.

The Maid dashes in leaving trays of salmon, potatoes, rice, and steamed vegetables before disappearing back into the kitchen. Maddie has given up on trying to learn her identity but doesn't like not having a way to refer to her, even in her own mind. She doesn't want to call her the Maid, so instead has taken to calling her Ruth, when she thinks of the woman.

She wants to talk to Ruth someday but has a suspicion the family would not like this and doesn't want to make trouble for her.

Maddie avoids looking at Emily directly. As she glances around the table, she realizes with a pang of guilt, that she's not the only one looking around and through the young woman. Billie Jo breaks the silence, "So, Mark, how was work today?"

Mark groans, "You would not believe who is at it again."

"Who? Oh, no, is it the save the trees people?" Billie Jo chuckles as she says this.

"They want people to have houses but don't want any trees cut, do they know where wood comes from?" Glen adds, with a saltiness Maddie hasn't heard from the typically quiet young man.

"Good one," Mark points to his future son-in-law. "It wasn't them this time. It was, oh, I don't remember their name, they're all kinda the same after a while. Want to hold up the permits because someone claims they saw a beaver nearby and if we don't tiptoe around them, they'll have the animal rights people from downstate descending on us."

Maddie's throat tightens. She waits a beat for the choking feeling to subside. She had never heard of Silver Spring before she ended up here accidentally. And she never knew of anyone downstate talking about such a place.

"Does that happen a lot?" Maddie asks. She doesn't want to challenge her host, but can't imagine buses of PETA activists from downstate heading for such a small target.

Mark smiles and she recognizes a patronizing look, "It hasn't happened yet. But that's because we protect ourselves here. And that includes you. You're one of us, dear, you have nothing to worry about."

Maddie wasn't worried. More confused. But she doesn't argue.

"People don't understand the sacrifices we have to make here in Silver Spring," Grandma Winnie stares into her glass of wine, as if convincing someone trapped at the bottom, not talking to people seated around her.

"It's a minor hold-up. Happens all the time. We'll win. We always do," Mark looks confident about this, cutting a piece of salmon and raising it to his mouth, he asks Emily, "how is the wedding planning coming along?"

"Mark," Grandma Winnie begins, giving her son a look Maddie thinks is intended to remind him to handle his oldest daughter with care still.

Emily seems unfazed, "It's going great, Dad. I've decided that Maddie is going to be my new Maid of Honor."

Maddie can't believe what she's hearing. It's not that Emily is sharing the news, which would happen eventually. It's the way she's saying it. As the younger woman continues, Maddie realizes her friend has changed. It was only two days ago Emily was obviously in deep grief. But as she tosses her blonde hair over her shoulder and shares the latest wedding plans, Maddie sees no sign of the despondent, hurting woman who walked with her only a few days ago.

Happy to see her friend is doing so much better, Maddie adds, "Yes, and when we get back up to speed on plans, we're going to get away to Lake Placid for a day, I know this great spa where…" she drifts into silence, realizing all eyes are on her. Billie Jo looks confused. Glen's face is stoic but even he reveals a hint of betrayal. Emily looks mortified.

After a moment of silence, Emily continues, "There is so much to do. The wedding is only four months away, I'll be lucky if I can venture as far as Orchid Street."

The family laughs. All except Desirae who looks Maddie in the eye with pity, as if to say, 'See? This is how things really are here.'

"Oh, sure, yes, I must have just been getting ahead of myself," Maddie backpedals, watching Emily, who gives a slight smile in agreement.

They visit at the dinner table later than usual that evening. Ruth comes several times to refresh tea, coffee, water, and for Grandma Winnie, wine. This, Maddie notices, is another new development. The older woman began drinking more in the days following Arianna's wedding. It seems to Maddie each night Grandma Winnie adds more, which she presumes can't be healthy for a woman her age.

Then again, she's an adult. She knows what's best for her, and if she wants to imbibe? More power to her. Why not enjoy your golden years?

By the time Emily and Glen say their goodbyes and leave, Mark has already gone upstairs to get ready for bed.

"A big presentation tomorrow, he needs his rest," Billie Jo explained. Desirae excused herself almost as soon as dinner was over, leaving only Grandma Winnie, Billie Jo, and Maddie.

"Grandma Winnie, you must be exhausted, let me help you up," Billie Jo offers as Maddie heads upstairs for the night.

"Oh, no, I can do it myself," Grandma Winnie replies, Maddie thinks she sounds grumpy, but it is late.

As she makes her way down the hall, she hears something else. She doesn't want to eavesdrop, but her ears picked out the sound of her name. She hesitates for a moment before starting upstairs.

"Are you sure about Maddie?" Grandma Winnie asks.

"She's fine. Dr. Needham saw to her himself... happened to be there," Billie Jo answers.

"Just can't believe it... not just one... both granddaughters... talking to a coach," she hears only parts of Grandma Winnie's reply. "If my Ralph were here... everything he worked for."

They continue to talk, but Maddie doesn't want to linger long in the stairway and besides, it sounds like whatever they had to say about her is done. She presumes that in Silver Spring, talking to a coach is stigmatized, like talking to a therapist is to many people still.

She doesn't see what the big deal is. Brushing her teeth and getting ready for bed, she notices her hair is growing longer now. It's almost long enough for spikey little pigtails. She's talked to therapists on and off. So has everyone she knows, at least before coming to Silver Spring.

CHAPTER 23

Maddie's eyes should be on the children assembled around the library table for arts and crafts. But she heard a familiar voice- his voice- a few moments ago and hasn't been able to concentrate since.

You're being silly, she thinks, feeling like a high school girl with a crush. She doesn't know David and has no reason to feel giddy when she hears him speaking in hushed tones behind the stacks of books in the library.

Yet here she is, training her ears to pick up any conversation. As if he his words have anything to do with her. From the meeting room, Maddie can only see a narrow section of aisles in the adjacent room. No matter how she focuses her eyes or cranes her neck, she will only see a shelf piled high with periodicals and another, the home of European History, A-M. She forces her mind away from David Croft, bringing her attention back into the meeting room.

The children have arranged themselves, as they always do, boys on the right side of the table, girls on the left. Their drawings are boxy and exaggerated. One girl, Tabitha, focuses on a drawing of a man, woman, and baby as if she is practicing surgery.

Next to her sits Maddie's boss's daughter, Laura. Laura carelessly colors a house purple and orange. Bold colors bleed from the door to the window to a rough sketch of a cat seated on the lawn.

Maddie walks behind the children, eyeing their handiwork, careful to reserve judgment or questions. She doesn't want to influence their creativity. Most of the drawings are of families, she notices. But one stands out.

Jessica is no older than the other kids, but she is one of a few who shows a natural talent for drawing. Maddie is used to her work being more refined than the other children. But today, it isn't the detail in the drawing that catches her eye, but the image on the center of the page.

A woman in an apricot gown. A wreath of leaves around her head. The woman in the drawing has red eyes, mouth stretched into a grimace.

Maddie's heart freezes.

She breathes deep, steadying herself.

"What is your drawing, Jessica?" She tries to sound casual but her voice shakes.

The child doesn't turn away from her drawing. She selects a black marker from the box and draws jagged lightning lines in the background.

"This is the Fall Bride, of course."

CHAPTER 24

The early spring afternoon is warmer today, and Maddie takes her time walking the few blocks from the Preservation Council office downtown to the Harris's home north of Silver Spring Park. She's only seen the perimeter of the park, vision obscured by shoulder-high stone walls and shrubs that form a solid evergreen boundary.

She approaches a park entrance and pivots, opting for the scenic route. The park is quiet. A path before her is framed by lawns on either side. Birds sing in the trees above her, their branches not yet in full bloom. Flowerbeds line the ground. Every few feet, a stone pedestal with a statue or bust. She stops to examine one. A plaque denotes the bust of Jeremiah Silver, one of the founders of Silver Spring and for whom the town was named. She notices the date of the town's founding; 1943.

A squirrel runs across the path, chased by another. They tussle before running up a tree. She continues to follow the path. Another pedestal and a bust, this one in bronze, bears a familiar name, Randolph "Ralph" Harris. She reads the tribute to Grandma Winnie's late husband. The final line catches her eye, "A man of pure intentions and pure blood."

She smiles, anticipating telling Grandma Winnie about stumbling upon the memorial to Ralph.

She turns the line over in her mind. A curious way to pay homage, she thinks.

She follows the sound of running water to a pond with a three-tier stone fountain in the center. Water cascades down one level to another before plunging into the pond. Ducks follow each other, swimming near the edge of the pond. Maddie approaches, a few of them honk and spread their wings, and retreat.

The sun casts shards of rainbows on the falling water. Maddie watches, mesmerized. The sound of honking brings her out of the momentary trance. A duck stands inches from her feet, wings at their side a proud and demanding look in their eye.

Maddie checks her bag, feeling around for the remnants of a snack, but finds nothing.

"Sorry, buddy. I'm all out."

The duck flaps their wings, hisses, and walks away.

Maddie heads toward the path, noticing a sign posted, 'Do not feed the ducks ANYTHING. We don't wish to encourage their nuisance to the town."

Maddie hasn't noticed the ducks posing any nuisance. She's seen signs like this posted in other parks, usually referring to bread or foods that can be harmful to the animals. She shivers, a pang of guilt makes her wish she had a snack to offer the critter. Just this once. No one would be around to know she broke the rules.

A golden filter stretches across the horizon behind the treetops. In the distance, Maddie can see the silhouettes of the tallest buildings downtown, those being only three stories high. Time has escaped her as she wandered through the park.

In the distance, a rabbit eyes her, darting beneath a bush when her footsteps come too close. The dirt path and lawns give way to downtown sidewalks and shops as she leaves the park. Young children race down the sidewalk, keeping out of earshot of their parents as they giggle to each other. A man on a bicycle smiles and waves as he rides past.

She rounds the corner from Main Street. Someone calls her name. She turns to see a familiar face. The young woman she's seen with David in the past. The woman waves, picking up her pace to catch up.

"It's Maddie, right?" she asks.

"Yes, and you're David's assistant? Gabrielle?"

Maddie doesn't need clarification, she just doesn't know what else to say in response. The young woman smiles, but Maddie sees something pass briefly over her face before it fades, and she adjusts to a friendly expression.

"I noticed you at the fountain, in the park," she begins, "and you looked so relaxed I didn't want to break your concentration. But then I saw you again just now and thought, well, us newbies have to stick together, right?"

Maddie blinks, willing her face to remove any sign of discomfort. Willing her eyes to stay relaxed, resisting the urge to show tell-tale signs of alarm. She didn't hear or see anyone else in the park. That someone saw her, unnoticed, is disconcerting.

"Oh, I must have been lost in thought. It's so beautiful," she looks around, desperate for an excuse to end the conversation.

"I guess, I mean, in a way." Gabriella shrugs and looks to the ground.

"You must have been there checking out the statues, right? For research?" Maddie ventures.

"Oh, right, the statues," Gabriella nods her head slowly. She opens her mouth like she wants to say something, but then hesitates.

"Oh, no, I hope I didn't say the wrong thing, I've never been into research and stuff, so I don't actually know what you do and I shouldn't have assumed," Maddie tries to correct herself.

"No, you're fine," Gabriella reassures her, "it's exactly what I do," she looks into the distance, "it's just that historic research… it's complicated. It's like that saying- there's three sides to every story. Yours, mine, and the truth."

"That's a new one for me, but, yeah it sounds about right."

"Well," Gabriella resumes eye contact, "I have the job of trying to sort out what is the truth; when sometimes all I have is one person's story or another."

"Oh, sure." Maddie adds, "So, what kinds of things are you studying? About Silver Spring? It's such an amazing place. I've never been any place like it."

Gabriella's brows furrow slightly, but as if self-conscious, she smiles, her eyes relax, erasing the tension Maddie thought she saw a moment ago. "Well, there aren't a lot of records. I mean, there aren't a lot of sources. So, I have a lot of archives told by the same people, but no records of," she hesitates as if struggling for words, "of other things."

Maddie isn't sure she understands. "Well, I work at the Preservation Council, I'm sure you could come look at our archives any time. My boss, Janice, she's pretty chill. Why don't you stop by?"

Gabriella smiles, but a rosy tint spreads across her cheeks and forehead. She puts her hands in her pockets and again looks to the ground, "Yeah, I know Janice," she exhales, "I appreciate the invitation, and honestly, I'd love to check out the archives. But I've had some," she pauses, "complications."

Now it's Maddie's turn to blush, "Oh, wow I keep putting my foot in my mouth today, I'm so sorry, I didn't even think there may be some issues before I said that. I keep forgetting that small towns have small-town politics."

"Are you from a small town?" Gabriella's eyes brighten.

"Wha-, um, not particularly. I mean, not a big city, but no, not like this. Um, sorry," she says between nervous giggles, "Actually, this sounds silly, but I wasn't expecting... I mean, I've been... since being here, I've been totally cut off from everything and I kind of forget being from anywhere else. Isn't that weird?"

"No," Gabriella's face is somber again, "not weird at all."

"And you know what else?"

"What's that?"

"I came here in December, and since then this is the first time anyone has asked me anything about my past."

"Don't you think that's weird?" Gabriella reflects Maddie's question back to her.

Maddie shrugs, "Nah, I mean why would anyone care about anyplace else if they live here."

Gabriella doesn't answer.

"But really, if there is a way I can get some information from the archives for you, just let me know. I mean if Janice hasn't been receptive, I've noticed she's weird about some things," Maddie trails off, overcome with a feeling she's saying too much.

It suddenly occurs to her she shouldn't be having this conversation.

"Like what?" Gabriella asks.

"Eh, you know, I really don't remember," she lies.

Gabriella nods, "Well, I don't want to make you late getting home. But please don't be a stranger. You know, like I said, us newbies have to look out for each other."

"Definitely, but we're probably better off here than anywhere else. I mean they don't even have police."

Gabriella raises her eyebrows, she nods, smiling but Maddie thinks there's more she wants to say.

"I'm staying at the Harris's, it's just a few blocks up this way, number 457, so stop by any time."

"Thanks," Gabriella grins.

Maddie turns the conversation around in her mind as she heads home. The younger woman's reaction to the statues was not what she expected. It reminds her of Desirae's hesitant responses the day of Arianna's memorial. But unlike Desirae, Maddie thinks Gabriella has her ducks in a row.

Do not feed the ducks ANYTHING

The sign flashes in Maddie's memory. She makes a note to herself to ask her new friend about this. And the statues.

There is a car parked in the driveway of the Harris household. She thinks, oh, we have company. But as she approaches, her heart races. It's her Acura. No sign of damage. It looks even better than it did before the accident.

Now you can leave, Carolyn's voice whispers.

No. My life is here now.

But maybe she'll convince Emily to venture out to Lake Placid, despite her recent excuses of being too busy with wedding planning.

CHAPTER 25

In her dream, Maddie enters the park again. This time, she wanders in through a cast iron gate woven in threads of morning glory vines. The gate creaks as she pushes it open, and a gust of wind urges her through the threshold.

Brown and red leaves somersault lightly against the ground ahead of her. Maddie walks in search of something. Urged forward by a vague sense that time is running out. In the distance, a woman approaches her. Maddie's blood turns to ice. The woman carries something in an outstretched hand and as she comes closer, Maddie recognizes her as Ruth, a covered tray in hand.

Maddie's shoulders relax. She's wanted to talk to Ruth. Needs to talk to her. The woman passes the tray to Maddie. She opens the lid, revealing the wooden dollhouse from Emily's room.

"Thank you," she turns to Ruth, but the woman is gone. The wind picks up.

You're running out of time," Carolyn chides her. She stands up ahead, by the fountain, dropping something to the ground again and again.

Maddie sets the tray on the ground, then hurries to her friend.

"Carolyn! I'm so glad you're here, look, I need to tell you, I miss …"

As she gets closer, she sees Carolyn holding a cluster of grapes, pulling one at a time from the bunch and dropping them to the ground. Ducks gather at her feet, pecking eagerly at the fruit, some toss the grapes into the air, catching them in their beaks. Her friend looks into the distance, through her, not at her.

"Carolyn, the sign says you're not supposed to…"

Carolyn's eyes snap into focus. She stares at Maddie, her eyes penetrating. Maddie steps backs, blinking.

"You need to be more careful," Carolyn warns.

"What do you mean? You mean the accident? I'm okay, no one got hurt, but…"

"There are three sides to every story," Gabrielle's voice is an echo, "yours, mine, and the Fall Bride."

Maddie's heart pounds. Questions race through her mind. She doesn't know where to start. A honk distracts her, she looks down to see ducks surrounding her feet, one rears back and flaps their wings.

She looks back to her friend, but Carolyn is gone. Maddie turns, looking for her friend. Her heart races. She can't breathe. There was more she had to ask, more she wanted to say to the woman friend who always guided her- who practically raised her after her father died.

She's gone.

Again.

Maddie's head spins. She drops to the ground, hands over her face, unable to stop the tears. Something brushes against her knee. She reaches a expecting to feel soft feathers, if the duck doesn't run away first. Instead, she feels fur, an arched body, and delicate bones.

She opens her eyes.

A rat stands on her knee.

She jumps to her feet as the creature squeals discontent.

The ducks are gone. In their place, rats gather around a feast of grapes. She turns to run, but there is no place to go. Rats surround her. They're closing in.

She wakes in a cold sweat.

Maddie catches her breath and slips from the unicorn bed and down the hall into the bathroom. She washes her face as quietly as possible. A creaking noise startles her. She turns off the faucet.

Another creak.

Back in the hallway, she follows the sound as far as Desirae's room. The creaking repeats, and she recognizes the sound as someone closing a window. Someone is breaking into the house.

She pushes the door open, bracing herself to confront a burglar. But the room is empty.

She exhales in relief.

Of course, it's empty, she reminds herself. Because here in Brigadoon no one locks their doors and there are no police.

Empty.

Which means Desirae is gone.

* * *

Maddie's stomach turns, could someone have taken the girl?

She slips into the room, eyes scanning for signs of struggle, but there are none.

Of course, because this is Silver Spring. There are no kidnappers, no burglars.

A breeze pushes against the curtains, they balloon into the room, revealing a window not quite fully closed.

Maddie didn't realize she was holding her breath until her tensed shoulders drop. She smiles.

Silver Spring doesn't have criminals. Just rebellious kids sneaking out at night.

She thinks of herself and Carolyn at Desirae's age as she approaches the window and peers out into the empty street. When she was Desirae's age, she was the only kid in her school without a cell phone. Even Carolyn had one, albeit an old flip phone kids used to make fun of her for carrying.

Maddie found much to resent about being poor. Wearing hand-me-downs, missing out on the school trip to France junior year, watching her classmates laugh and repeat lines from movies she wouldn't see until they came out on video months later.

But one advantage she did have in her remnant of poverty-induced analog life was not being trackable. She recalls the grin on Carolyn's face when she would show up at her friend's house, tapping on her window then ducking behind a bush. She would wait, the mosquitos buzzing in her ears and under her eyes, holding her breath in the still nights. It was only a few minutes, she knew, but felt like forever before the window would creak and she would see Carolyn's sneaker, then a leg, then the rest of her friend emerge from the side of the house. They would hold hands and run through the lawns together.

Back in the unicorn bed, her memory continues as she stares at the Emily's old dollhouse. Where had they even gone that seemed so important then? Nowhere special. To the park. Sometimes to the basketball court where the uncool but irresistible skateboarding kids hung out until the early morning hours.

Sometimes they met other friends and indulged in a wine cooler or beer if someone could find one. Thinking of it now, Maddie realizes there was nothing they did in the wee hours of the morning that couldn't have been just as easily done on a Saturday afternoon. But the thought of running through the streets at night, anonymous amidst the shadows, had been a thrill.

Talking about the boys they liked or teachers they hated was more exciting at two in the morning than on the walk home from school on a Thursday.

She thinks Desirae has discovered the same secret. When you're a kid, everything is more fun at night. Then you grow up and realize the mysterious liminal hours are nothing but a chance to freeze to death in a car, parked among other homeless in a Wal Mart parking lot.

She should tell Billie Jo. Or Emily. Shouldn't she?

She sees her younger self sitting on a sweatshirt painting her toenails while Carolyn eats popcorn.

"I heard a rumor," Carolyn had told her between bites, "Sophia said Mr. Bowers got arrested for having kid porn on his computer at school."

"He acts like a pedo, so, sure. He probably did."

"I like his new substitute teacher better anyway."

They had gossiped. Occasionally picking flowers in the park and using them as improvised microphones to sing pop songs or show tunes.

And yes, there had been pedos. Like their math teacher Mr. Bowers. But he was at school. In the park, they would see an occasional person staring vacantly into the night, but no one every bothered them.

And besides, this is Silver Spring. There is no safer place on earth for kids to meet at a park at night to gossip and paint their nails or watch skateboarders.

As she drifts to sleep Maddie resolves to talk to Desirae tomorrow. Discreetly.

CHAPTER 26

The next day at work, Maddie is swamped with requests complicated further by the photocopier repeatedly breaking down. For the first time, she can't wait to leave the office.

The memory of Desirae's partially open window and her intention to talk to the girl have subsided. Until she feels a cold hand grip her arm as she's walking home from work.

She jumps, screaming in fear as she turns to see Desirae. Her panicked reaction makes the child jump as well, a hand raising to her chest as she tries to catch her breath.

"I'm sorry," Desirae seems genuinely remorseful for scaring her, but there is something else, an intensity, in the child's eyes.

She's unpredictable, Maddie thinks. Maybe she should worry about her sneaking off at night. Her judgment isn't the best.

"Sorry," Desirae repeats, looking cautiously side to side. "I didn't want to scare you, but I tried calling your name and you seemed lost in thought, and I wanted to catch you before we got home."

Maddie's breathing has almost settled to normal. She smiles, trying to downplay how uneasy she feels. Why? Desirae is just a kid. Like she was, right?

Except the tantrums. And the weird coach thing. Whatever that is.

"I wanted to try to catch you too," Maddie looks around, no one else is in earshot. A mother and her child stroll down the block several feet away. An older man has just left the post office, but he's walking in the opposite direction.

Desirae motions for her to keep walking.

"I wanted you to know, Desirae," Maddie begins, but Desirae cuts her off.

"Please, call me Rae, but only when it's just us."

"I need to tell you, sorry to cut you off, but I need to tell you, before you say anything," Rae has circled in front of her now and turns to block her path. Maddie's heart races.

"I know you came into my room last night."

Maddie freezes, unsure what to say or how to respond. She can't deny it. And besides, why would she?

Rae continues, "It's fine. I'm fine, just wanted you to know. You don't have to worry about me running off and doing crazy shit."

Maddie isn't entirely convinced, but before she can say anything Rae continues, "You may think you have to tell on me, because of some like adult code of ethics, or whatever. But I just want you to know I know about you."

Maddie blinks, her jaw drops.

"What do you mean?"

"I know about you," Rae repeats. "The stuff my mom gave back to you, it wasn't everything. You know it. I know it. I don't know how much my mom knows, but I know about you. I know you had no place to go. I know there's a reason you're not in a hurry to leave here. And I know what the reason is."

Maddie tries to form words but her lips feel numb. She shakes her head. *Is this blackmail? Is Rae threatening her?*

"I don't know… what… I mean, what are you…?"

"Look, I'm not going to say shit to anyone okay? Tell anyone here whatever you want about your past, I won't get involved. But I need you to promise you won't rat me out."

The word makes her think of the rat crawling down the side of the dollhouse. At the Christmas party. At Ariana's wedding.

"I, Rae, I'm an adult…"

"Yeah, and you have secrets too, right? Explains why you passed out at City Council that night. I'll keep your secret if you keep mine. Promise?"

Maddie blinks again, trying to regain some kind of upper hand. "Where are you going at night? How often are you…"

"I'll tell you at some point. I promise. But not now."

"Tell me the truth, are you going out to drink? To use drugs? I won't judge you I just want to make sure you're safe…"

Rae rolls her eyes, shaking her head, "No, nothing like that. I swear," right hand raised in an oath, "and when you find out you'll laugh for thinking it was anything like that. I promise."

"Well, is it a boy?"

Something passes over Rae's face. She looks away, cheeks flushing red.

"No, it's not a boy, it's not like that."

"Are you going out alone? Are you with someone else? What if something happens to you and no one knows where you are?"

Rae looks side to side, hands raised in a gesture of reassurance.

"It's a girl, okay? I can tell you that much. And some other friends. We're not drinking, we're not partying. I promise. Just stuff they wouldn't approve of here."

Maddie sees the pleading look in the child's eyes.

Rae.

But only in secret.

Coaching.

Maddie remembers the drama over Rae's boots.

Looks at Rae's hair.

Maddie stares, not meaning to, as reality crystalizes.

Why hadn't she noticed sooner?

"Rae, is this about who you are? As a person? Not how your family, or this town sees you?"

Rae's face reddens. The child looks away.

"Is… .is that why they make you see a…. a coach?"

Rae pulls her fingers through her uneven hair, she breathes heavily and Maddie wonders if she's gone too far.

"There's a lot you don't know about. And that's part of it but it isn't all of it." Rae's words come rapidly, voice lowered, "I'll tell you more someday, I will. I think you're cool, or at least not a narc, but you have to promise me, promise me you won't say anything."

Rae opens her eyes again. On the verge of tears.

Maddie had friends growing up who were gay and some who later came out as trans or nonbinary. She knew it was a sensitive and sometimes traumatic experience. And that things had only gotten worse, especially in places like Texas and Tennessee. But she didn't think it was bad in New York.

Then again, Silver Spring was different.

"Are there also," she chooses her words carefully, "different pronouns you want me to use? When it's just us?"

Rae smiles, "They and them. When no one else is here."

Rae grins ear to ear and Maddie's heart sinks. She thinks of the Queer Kids Club from high school. Recalls the Queer Prom she went to as an ally to her friends. For the first time in years she remembers the Rainbow Cat, an artsy hangout in her old neighborhood that was a safe haven. And that was in Poughkeepsie. In Silver Spring, there was nothing. And she realizes it will probably stay that way for a long time.

Maybe they'll change with the times. It's not a bad place…

Maddie smiles, trying to be encouraging without the patronizing tone people take toward teens.

"Hey, it's okay. I won't say anything. Just promise you'll be safe, okay?"

"Oh, you don't have to worry about that. We, there are others, we know how to be safe. About everything."

"What do you mean?"

Rae runs the edge of their sleeve over their eyes and stifles a sniffle. They look around again before answering.

"Because if anything were to happen, and I mean anything, that leads to anyone other than you finding out? I'm dead."

CHAPTER 27

May 1 2023

Maddie hasn't driven her car since it was returned. Her initial excitement dissipated into indifference. She strolls down the block from the Preservation society to get a sandwich from the corner deli.

"Don't hurry back, it's too sunny a day to waste indoors, and we're caught up on most of the important things," Janice told her when she went on her lunch break, usually an hour at noon.

The sun lights Maddie's face, a welcome contrast from the windowless office where she spent the morning compiling images for the posters and slideshows the preservation council planned for the centennial celebration.

Maddie reaches for the door to the deli, but it swings open before she can grab the handle. A young woman with wavy dark hair backs out of the deli, her face almost concealed behind a full paper bag which she holds from the bottom.

"Oh, Maddie, I'm sorry."

She recognizes Gabriella's voice.

"No worries," Maddie replies. "I've actually been hoping to run in to you," she adds.

"Really? What's up?" Gabriella asks.

An older couple saunters past, hand in hand. A week ago, Maddie would have found them charming, but their presence makes her uncomfortable now.

"Actually," Maddie hesitates, "are you on break? Do you want to walk through the park?"

Gabriella follows Maddie's gaze toward the couple, and other townspeople who pass by. "I would love to walk through the park. I'm not in a hurry, but," she looks around, then leans closer, "I have another idea, grab your lunch," she motions toward the deli, "and I'll meet you out here."

"Eh, I'm not that hungry," Maddie replies.

"Well, I have more than enough, so if you change your mind, you can have some of mine. Come," she nods in the direction of the library.

Maddie follows. After her conversation with Rae, she has felt bolder. But there is something else, something she can't put her finger on, that has been haunting her.

She thinks Gabriella is leading her to the library, but the younger woman makes an abrupt turn down an alley, before turning again, now backtracking in the direction she just came but on a narrow path behind the row of buildings that she thinks was once a side street . . Gabriella leads her in the direction of a what looks like a garage.

The garage has windows and Maddie thinks it may have been converted into an in-law apartment behind one of the many bungalows. A small yard separates it from neighboring buildings. Lilacs are in full bloom. She inhales, taking in the light scent

"Is this your place?" Maddie asks, as Gabriella unlocks the door and leads her inside.

"That's one way of putting it."

She walks inside. Maddie starts to follow her but almost walks into her. She watches the younger woman pull the shades and curtains closed and turn on a flashlight, scanning the room. She does this three times.

When Gabriella seems content that the flashlight has done its job, she turns it off and switches on a lamp. The room is lined with stacks of books and old newspapers. Not an in-law apartment, she realizes, there is no furniture to speak of. Gabriella drops her bag on the floor and returns to the door, locking it behind them.

"You lock your door?"

"Uh-huh," Gabriella answers, her back still to her guest.

Maddie's stomach tightens, was this a mistake? She watches the younger woman dart around the room, peering out the windows before pulling the blinds and curtains closed again.

Mismatched cushions on the floor serve as the makeshift chairs. She recognizes the vintage upholstery of one of the cushions. It's the same pattern as a couch Maddie had in one of over a dozen places she and her mother called home between the year her father died and her first apartment three years later.

"This might seem weird," Gabriella begins, her voice apologetic, "but you need to know there are cameras downtown and in the park. There could be cameras on us when we came in, but I doubt it. If there were, I would have heard about it by now. But just assume," Gabriella sits on one of the cushions, "that there are always eyes on you. There's literally nowhere you can go and speak near downtown where people aren't watching you.

Maddie crosses her legs and lowers herself to the ground, sitting on the cushion across from the younger girl. She considers this, "I guess that makes sense, I mean they need to keep an eye on things, in case there are robberies or vandalism?"

Gabriella doesn't respond. Maddie changes the subject.

"So, Gabrielle, how did you come to be in Silver Spring?"

Gabriella sweeps papers and dust aside clearing a spot on the floor. She begins to unpack the paper bag. Maddie eyes the room, it's not gross but it's also not clean. Her friend must be hungry.

"You're going to think this is crazy," she opens a container of salad and holds a plastic fork to Maddie, who declines with a shake of her head, "I still don't think it makes any sense. But, I was a student. At Skidmore, and I received an invitation to intern at a place near here," she balances the salad on her lap and proceeds to stab at small chunks of lettuce, "and since I don't drive, I took a train. But," she pauses to chew quickly, "and this is where it's crazy, the train had a layover. So, I got out at the station, went to a restroom, came out of the station, and…" Gabriella looks into the distance, she shakes her head as if unable to accept what happened next, "the densest fog I've ever seen, like where you can't see what is right in front of you? It was everywhere."

Maddie nods.

"I couldn't see the bench outside the train station I was sitting on like ten minutes before that. If I didn't have my suitcase with me? I don't think I would have been able to find that either."

Maddie has seen fog like this, she recalls a visit to Lake George during college. She had to pull the car over because it was impossible to see the road. When the fog lifted, she realized she miscalculated a safe parking spot along a curb and was parked, flashers on, in the right lane of a road.

"I saw a silhouette, or I thought I did, and I followed them. But then I lost them. And I was just wandering. I slipped, I think? I couldn't even tell. I think I slipped. And next thing I remember, I was walking around on Grove Street."

The room is still.

Gabriella eats another forkful of salad, the crunch of lettuce echoes in the room.

"Crazy, right?"

"I would have thought so," Maddie begins, "but…"

"But you ended up here by accident," Gabriella interrupts, still chewing.

Maddie thinks of the sunflower sliding out of her sight behind the fence. An accident. No. This had been a fortunate turn of events. Mostly.

"I mean, yes, I didn't plan to come here. But… It was weird."

She hopes the woman will tell her more, but instead, Gabriella pops the tab on a soda and begins drinking, as if to indicate Maddie has the floor.

"I was on my way to a job interview," she holds her hand out in Gabriella's direction, affirming the connection in their stories. "And I pulled off the road, for some reason," it occurs to her the events have become hazy.

Foggy.

"Oh, I was looking for a restroom," she suddenly recalls. "And something happened, I think the sun was in my eyes. And," her eye widen, she slams her hand down on her thigh, "sorry, I just remembered, I saw someone too."

Gabriella pauses, fork midair.

"I saw this person in an apricot dress. In winter. No coat or anything. With a weird flower crown," her voice becomes louder, her words come faster as she remembers, "and I lost control of the car but the thing is," she pauses, pointing a finger in the air as if it helps her recall the details, "the thing is, every time I mention her, everyone gets all quiet, I was sure I hit this person," tears well in Maddie's eyes, her voice begins to choke, "but no one else acknowledges she exists. And I even saw her again a few days later, but it's like I'm hallucinating."

Gabriella returns her fork to the salad, holding the sides of the container with both hands.

"My car was in the shop for months, and the Harris's just took me in and have been so wonderful, like they made me feel right at home …"

"Except you haven't been able to find your phone," Gabrielle adds.

"You too?"

Gabriella smiles. "You really like it here."

"Don't you?"

Gabriella continues eating her salad, she twists her mouth to the side as if considering how to answer. "I can see why you would like it. I can see why some people would think it's the perfect place to live…"

"But?"

Gabriella looks into the distance, "But, I've had different experiences. So, there are things that stand out to me, but wouldn't stand out to you."

"What do you mean?"

"My real name isn't Gabrielle. It's *Gabriella*. But here, it's like they all decided for me that my name is Gabrielle, for one."

Maddie nods, recalling the nickname others decided for her as well. And something else. Rae, hiding behind an unwanted given name.

"Should I call you that? Do you prefer Gabriella?" Maddie asks, recalling the look on Rae's face when the child heard Maddie use their chosen name.

"My family is Peruvian and Dominican, so I'm more of an outsider than the average outsider. It's easier, no, safer, to just go along. *Gabrielle* is less threatening to them."

Maddie sits back in her cushion, eyes wide, "have people here been racist to you?"

Gabriella taps her hand on the sides of her salad container as she explains, "I grew up in Glens Falls, so I can hold my own in white spaces, exhausting as it can be," she leans to the side, resting one hand on the floor at her side, "Are they racist? Sure, yes. But so is every white town."

Maddie wants to interrupt, to reassure her it can't be true of every white town because not all white people are racist. Something Carolyn used to argue with her about all the time. But her instincts tell her to listen.

"It's more than that," Gabriella continues, "I won't say it's worse, but it's like, there's another layer to it. Take my word for it, my radar is up in a way yours isn't and I notice things you don't notice."

Maddie's heart sinks. She doesn't want to see Silver Spring as a bad place, they've been so good to her.

She recalls the Council meeting. Sees Dr. Needham speaking at the microphone, demanding they lock up homeless people. Then hovering above her, concerned. Genuinely worried.

She shakes her head slowly.

Gabriella continues, "There's more to Silver Spring than just white people having white people biases. And I think, I mean something tells me you sense it. You know it."

"It's such a beautiful place, though," Maddie begins, but the words seem hollow. "I mean, I just don't understand. They're all so nice.

But then at the meeting? The way they were talking about Green-ridge… and that's why I wanted to talk to you."

Gabriella tilts her head, encouraging Maddie to continue.

"I have learned some things. But not a lot, I mean I still have so many questions. And I thought maybe you would know, but more importantly," she meets Gabriella's eyes, "maybe you under-stand. Because you're not from here and because," she motions to the windows, the locked door, "I mean, you seem to know more than I do about this. I mean, you see it. Because Emily… she doesn't see it. But Desirae does."

Gabriella looks confused.

"I caught Ra- I mean, um, Desirae, sneaking out a few weeks ago. I don't know where she's going. She made me swear secrecy. Got all freaked out about it. I mean, what kid doesn't sneak around as a teen? But she was acting like it was some kind of life and death thing if she gets caught."

Gabriella leans forward, her eyes wide, concerned. "Don't tell me the details."

Maddie scoffs. "I think everyone's taking things a little too seri-ously. I mean there are some quirky habits, but isn't that part of what makes small towns quaint?"

"If Desirae is freaked out, it's for good reason," Gabriella responds, "even you know something is off. You know it. That's why you wanted to talk to me."

Maddie drops her gaze. She nods her head, recognizing it's true. After a moment, she adds, "And there's another thing did you go to Arianna's Memorial."

Gabriella lowers her eyes, she nods, "I did."

"Desirae was really upset. Like she was crying. And she seemed to think Arianna may have been killed. Said something about how she was going to bail on the wedding. But no one else talks about it."

"Someone mentioned it, in passing, at Town Council," Gabriella points out.

"You're right," Maddie forgot that detail. "And the crazy thing is, I think even Emily suspects something. But she… she started to open up to me one day, we were on a walk, actually it was the first day we met, and she started to talk to me, but it was like… like she had more to say but then shut down. And then after that, it's like she's obsessed with wedding plans."

Maddie pauses, folding her hands on the table, "And I'm glad she has something to keep her motivated, but it's almost like…"

"Like a cult."

Maddie feels the room fall away. She lifts her head, eyes wide, and meets Gabriella's gaze. Time stands still.

"Yes. It never occurred to me but yes," Maddie rubs the heel of her hand against her forehead.

"There's a lot we have to catch up about," Gabriella begins, "but we have to be more careful than you realize. I mean, really, really not take for granted how much surveillance goes on here. This may be hard for you, Maddie, but trust me. Don't take for granted that you are safe here."

"What do you mean?"

"I'm not sure exactly. I haven't figured it out yet, but there is something weird here."

"I mean, yeah, there are some quirky things, but danger?"

"You just said yourself, something odd happened with Arianna and no one is talking about it. There's a lot more no one is talking about. And I want you to know some of the things I've uncovered, but not today. We don't have time."

Maddie nods.

"Act normal, go about business as usual, don't draw attention. David mentioned you guys have a date for lunch with Emily and Glen?"

"It's, um, I don't know if it's a date, but…" Maddie blushes.

"Well, whatever it is, have fun. Blend in, just like you have already. But be careful what you say."

"You don't think David is bad, do you?"

Gabriella pauses, studies her fingernails, then replies, "I don't know that it's a matter of being bad per se, but there's a culture here …"

Cult. Culture. It occurs to Maddie for the first time the two words are linked. She nods her head as Gabriella continues.

"David, so far, appears to be part of that culture. And we need to be careful until we have evidence otherwise. As far as I can tell, you and Desirae are the only ones in Silver Spring who aren't… aren't like everyone else."

"What about Arianna?"

Gabriella bites her lower lip, "That's a whole thing. A whole conversation. We need to put a pin in that for next time."

Maddie nods.

"Let's meet again, at lunchtime."

"Tomorrow?"

"Too soon. Let's say," Gabriella looks up as if an invisible calendar hovers above them, "let's plan for Friday."

"Okay. I'll meet you at the deli?"

"No, Let's meet at the park that day, but we'll come here again. And remember, downtown is full of cameras," she hesitates, "and it's possible the residential neighborhoods are, too."

Maddie's heart races. "We've already been sneaking out."

"Right. And it's possible someone already knows, or not. Assume they do. Until you reach the town line, act as if you know you are being watched."

Maddie nods. This is probably over the top, she thinks. But maybe not.

"Here," Gabriella gives Maddie a sandwich wrapped in white deli paper. "Eat this on the way back, or part of it. If anyone asks you got carried away birdwatching or something."

Maddie agrees.

"And Maddie," Gabriella adds as she walks toward the door, "I'm glad we got a chance to talk today."

CHAPTER 28

Gabriella

Gabriella didn't want to open up to Maddie. She didn't want to make friends with anyone here. But something deep in her gut compelled her to. It wasn't attraction. Not the feeling she had when she met Brenda, a random encounter at a bus station, followed by another chance meeting in a coffee shop weeks later.

It wasn't the same, but then, it wasn't entirely different. Something, some unknown force made Gabriella feel like she needed to talk to the young woman alone. Maybe it's because they are the only two outsiders.

Don't get it twisted, a voice in the back of her mind challenged her. *Push comes to shove, you're the outsider.*

She knows it's true. Knew it even as she brought Maddie to the garage. But it felt good to finally talk to someone. Not like the way she talks to David, mostly business, not personal. Of course, she didn't really tell Maddie anything. Not the worst of what she learned. She wants to, but it's too soon.

What's the harm in testing the waters? Aside from sounding crazy, it was no secret she arrived with the fog one day. Gabriella doesn't want to get comfortable with the idea, but it seemed like Maddie really wanted to talk to her. Like maybe she had a hint that something was off.

Not that she understood. Not truly. But she's from the real world, which is how Gabriella came to think of everywhere outside of Silver

Spring. She must see it. The sexism. The creepy Donna Reed world. The obsession with weddings and obedience. The servants. She must see it. Gabriella is certain. And if she's not perfect, at least she may be teachable.

CHAPTER 29

Maddie

Maddie can't remember the last time she went on a date. She looks around the restaurant, searching for any sign of David, while pulling at the curly hair, no longer spikes, now closer to ringlets, at the nape of her neck. David hasn't arrived yet. She wonders if it is intentional.

"He's notorious for always being late," Emily reassures her, looking over her shoulder to Glen for confirmation.

Glen nods, twirling his straw and staring into the glass of water as the trio sits at the booth near the back corner of the town's pizzeria.

The location was Maddie's idea. Emily wanted to meet at Mrs. Warren's restaurant, but Maddie didn't want anything too formal. She already had a sinking feeling Emily was more optimistic about their compatibility.

They've been waiting ten minutes. Long enough for Emily to give Maddie a tour, pointing out the historic black and white photos framed and hanging on the wall, and to show off the jukebox- an original- stocked with songs that were popular in the days of drive-ins and roller-skates.

"Did I mention," Emily begins, gently grabbing Maddie's arm, "David speaks Latin. He actually speaks three," she turns to Glen, "was it three languages honey?"

Glen puts an arm around Emily, "I think three languages, yes," he leans in and kisses Emily, then adds, "If I didn't know any better, I would think you wanted to marry David and were just marrying me for my good looks," he smiles and kisses her again.

"He's joking," Emily explains, unnecessarily.

A bell signals the door opening, to her relief, it's David. She isn't being stood up. But as he sits at their booth, next to her, her anxiety surges again. She didn't realize how much she enjoyed not worrying about impressing a man. When it no longer seemed a prospect, she felt some relief. But now, that old tension returns. She feels like she's under a microscope.

Sneaking a glance to the side, she notices David isn't even looking at her. Not directly.

"Hi, sorry I'm late," he glances in her direction, then faces Emily and Glen, shifting his gaze from side to side. Maddie thinks he looks as nervous as she feels. It never occurred to her that a guy would be nervous about going on a date.

"No worries, I had a chance to show Maddie around, so it's all good."

The server returns, but only with two menus. Before Maddie can ask for an additional two, she's gone. She eyes Emily and Glen, who open their menu as if they are used to sharing one. David follows suit. Maddie scans the items on the menu. Her stomach clenches.

This must be a joke.

She looks up, expecting some reaction. Emily studies the options, tracing the words with her finger. Glen rubs her back, moving her head from side to side as if he is considering his options, but nothing about his expression shows alarm.

She ventures a glance at David, who sits solemnly, tapping his lip with his finger as he reads the menu. She can see a list of headings followed by descriptions for each type of pizza.

So, it's that kind of place, she thinks, recalling the trend of naming casual dining entrees after movie stars or television characters that crept up at some point in the last ten years, as far as she could recall.

"This place uses the funny names, I see," Maddie remarks casually.

Emily furrows her brow, she lifts her menu and flips it over, as if looking for a hidden clue, then turns it back, shrugs, and shakes her head, "I don't know what you mean."

"The names? I mean, the pizza names?" Maddie feels heat flood her cheeks.

"Oh, I keep forgetting you're new. I'm so used to you being part of the family," David replies, then turns to Emily, "I learned about this from Gabrielle, apparently," he leans over the table, passing his hand over the menu," people from away aren't used to this because in other places, people call their food… well, they just call it what it's made of."

Emily and Glen lean back in unison. Their faces stoic. Glen drops his gaze then looks to the side, Emily clears her throat and continues looking at the menu.

Tears burn in Maddie's eyes. She's hurt, but also angry. He's talking about her like she's a specimen to be studied, not someone sitting at the table beside him.

Maddie thinks they'll drop the topic, but Glen looks at her, brows furrowed, and asks, "so, if you want a Father Dearest, you just call it a dough with sauce, cheese, and pepperoni?"

"No," Maddie tries to control her voice. She's close to tears but also wants to yell. "No, we call it pizza. But we just call it pepperoni pizza."

"What do you call a First Child? You don't actually call it a mushroom, sausage, and pepper pizza, do you?" Glen counters.

Why is he being such an ass?

Maddie leans over David's arm, no longer concerned about personal space. She reads the lists of campy names and ingredients.

First Child- a very special dish made with love and anticipated by all. Ingredients: dough, tomato sauce, cheese, mushroom, peppers, and sausage.

"Um, yes."

She feels the table vibrate slightly and realizes Emily's leg is shaking.

"Well, I mean there are some things that we give names to, like for example there's a sandwich called a Ruben."

"Who's Ruben?" Emily asks, her leg suddenly still.

Maddie blinks, "I don't know. I could Goo-" she stops, remembering as she reaches for her phone that no, she can't Google it. "I mean, I don't know. It's just a sandwich. It's got sauerkraut, Russian dressing, and either corned beef or turkey, but technically the turkey one is called a Rachel," Maddie trails off, realizing she's rambling.

"But you don't call them something meaningful? Only random names?"

Maddie starts to feel shame, as if she invented food naming conventions, but shakes her head, "What? No, it's, I mean it's just food. We don't treat it like, like a message. It's just a pizza or a taco, or a sandwich."

"What's a taco?" Glen asks.

"Um, it's a, it's like a, you know. Like Taco Tuesday?"

She's met with blank stares.

"Well," she tries to find common ground, "there is a trend since I was a kid where some places give fun names to their meals, so it's kind of like this? They name the food after, like shows, or movie characters, or other pop culture stuff."

"Hmmm," Emily nods slowly and looks down, then turns to Glen, "I think I'll have the Respected Mayor."

Glen smiles, "Oh, I love the Respected Mayor. Good choice. "I'm going to have a Beautiful Bride," he smiles, leaning in for another kiss.

Maddie glances down at the menu. Sure enough, it's under the Town Founder.

Beautiful Bride: A delightful dish everyone loves. Dough prepared free of garlic or anything offensive, topped with delicious cheese, pure and perfect.

"What about you?" David asks.

Maddie is relieved to be off the food-naming conversation. The weird names and descriptions make the prospects less tempting. She looks down at the menu and recites the first item she sees.

"The Bossy Wife," she doesn't register the words until she's said them and wants to take it back.

"Uh-oh, David, better watch out, you've got yourself a bossy bride to be," Glen teases.

Crimson floods David's cheeks.

Maddie reads the description.

The Bossy Wife: sourdough topped with garlic, onions, tomato sauce, and aged provolone cheese. Doused with pepper and dotted with olives, too much of this meal will give you a bellyache.

Good God.

David clears his throat. Looks around the room and turns to Maddie, his voice artificially upbeat, "So, this restaurant was built in 1947."

Maddie looks into his hazel eyes, grateful for the distraction. "Really?" She hopes she doesn't sound too eager.

"Yes. Yes. It was a town Meeting Hall until the late 1980s. But when it was the Meeting Hall," David points in the direction of the Juke Box, "that area used to be where the Founders would meet and discuss town business.

Maddie follows his gaze as he turns to another part of the pizzeria, a wall decorated with framed black and white photos from past eras.

"This over here," he continues, "was a bar."

"Because you should never talk business without a few drinks," Glen raises his glass of water, mimicking a toast.

They laugh. Maddie is relieved that her blunder has been upstaged by David's knowledge of local history.

The server arrives, staring intently at her steno pad.

"Everyone ready?"

"I think so," Glen nods, then continues to order, "I'll have a Wise Grandfather, and my wife-to-be," he gestures to Emily, "will have a Respected Mayor."

Emily beams.

Maddie doesn't understand why Emily doesn't speak for herself. Before she can add her order, David begins, "I'll have a Happy Developer," he eyes Glen, who smiles at the homage to his profession, "and my date will have a Bossy Wife."

The server looks up for the first time, gives Maddie a sly grin, and collects the menus, darting away before Maddie can say anything.

Maddie understands. She doesn't need to ask. As chatty as Emily and Billie Jo and even Grandma Winnie are at home around the dinner table, when in public, men order for them.

* * *

Later that night as she waits for sleep to take hold, Maddie stares at the wooden dollhouse that was once Emily's. She replays the date in her mind. David is good-looking. And she enjoyed talking to him about his work.

"The man is an encyclopedia," Emily commented on the way home, "he's a good match for you, the smartest guy in town," she turns to Glen," I mean you know what I mean. When it comes to history smarts, not like engineering and real estate smarts."

Later that evening, sitting on the edge of the bed, Maddie replays the date in her mind, studying the dollhouse across from her. A week ago, Maddie would have enjoyed the attention and the insinuations that they were already a couple. She would have even overlooked the gross pizza names or having a man order for her.

But.

She sees a hairline crack running down the side of the dollhouse. Was it there before?

Her eyelids grow heavy. Maddie leans back into the softness of the unicorn bed, surrounded by pillows. She blinks, her eyes losing focus on the shadows on the canopy overhead.

Does it really matter? She thinks. It's just a pizzeria. Don't let it ruin everything you have.

Carolyn's voice responds from the recesses of her mind, but she's already asleep.

CHAPTER 30

Madison sleeps heavily during the nights following her double date with David, Glen, and Emily. While Rae slips out the bedroom window down the hall, Madison slips into a dream, or what Carolyn used to call, another plane. In this dream, Maddie visits the ethereal pizzeria to the scent of garlic, heavy in the air.

Someone ordered a Bossy Wife. It's funny in the dream. She follows the sounds of laughter to a booth in the far corner. Carolyn sits at the table beside Grandma Winnie, and David.

Madison's mother is there. Nonchalant, seated among her new friends.

"Hey, sorry I'm late," she slides into the booth beside her mother. In the way of dreams, it doesn't occur to her to be surprised the woman is alive. She doesn't hug her mother the way she swore she would if she had the chance one more time.

When her spectral mother pulls her close for a peck on the cheek, it doesn't occur to her to be anything but embarrassed.

"I was just telling David we have your princess room all set up at home. For after the wedding. You can live with us, you know. As long as you want," Grandma Winne beams.

"Oh, wedding?" She looks to David, then glances at her finger. No ring. Why are they talking about weddings?

"Oh, thank you but that won't be for years to come. I'm not giving up my unicorn bed any time soon."

They laugh, as if indulging a naïve child.

Madison turns to her mother, "What are you going to have?"

Her mother flips the menu open, her eyes dart across the page as she scans top to bottom. "I'll have the Dead Daughter," she responds casually, closing the menu.

Madison's heart pounds. Her lips suddenly dry, she must have heard wrong.

"I'm sorry, the what?"

"The Dead Daughter," her mother turns to face her, a slight smile. That's when Madison notices the change in her mother's eyes. The distance. The icy dimness that was never there before, no matter how far she fell from her radiant self.

"That's not funny," Madison feels tears well in her eyes. She reaches for the menu an flips it open, nearly tearing the frayed binding. She scans the names of entrees.

The Incorrigible Bastard…

The Disobedient Servant…

And there it was. The Dead Daughter. Madison's stomach turns. She starts reading the ingredients but a shadow cast over the table distracts her. She looks up as David began reciting orders for everyone at the table.

"Are you going to let him order for you, Carolyn?" she asks, incredulous.

Her friend turns to her with the same blank stare as her mother, "It's too late for me, dear. The question is, will you?"

Grandma Winnie interrupts, "He better order for you," she eyes Madison while nudging David in the ribs too hard to be playful.

"I don't want you to order for me, I can order for myself," Madison reaches for the menu but David's hand comes down hard over hers.

"You don't understand," his face is still real, not glossed over with the frozen expression the others had.

"Sir, your order? You need to complete your order." She turns to Madison, "Miss, am I to assume you're ordering the Dead Fiancée?"

Madison recoils from David. The room darkens. She tries to answer but her voice sticks in her throat, she looks to Carolyn for help, but the woman only returns a blank stare. She turns to David one last time, but where he sat a moment ago, between Grandma Winnie and the friend who practically raised her, is Arianna's corpse. Her wedding dress torn and streaked with blood.

Madison opens her mouth to scream, but can only produce a futile retching noise.

"Miss, your order," she hears in the background, followed by something else, a faint sound. Squeaking. A shadow moves somewhere behind Arianna's head, it creeps forward, small at first, then growing. The mass crawls out from behind Arianna's neck, stretches its front paws to lean against her collarbone, and scuttles down the front of her dress, long pink tail trailing across the ruined gown as the rat launches itself onto the table and ran toward Madison.

She forces herself to scream but wakes with a start instead.

107

Maddie's stomach turns. She doesn't have to glance at the clock to know it's eleven thirty. She knows by the smell coming from Janice's office. Her boss brought lunch from home, tuna sandwiches on whole wheat bread with a side of macaroni salad and fruit punch to drink.

It's Janice's Thursday lunch. Typically, the scent of her boss's lunch; ravioli and garlic bread on Monday, shepherd's pie on Tuesday, leftover meatloaf on Wednesday, and baked salmon and scalloped potatoes on Friday, remind Maddie that it's time for her to take a break and walk down to the deli. Or follow the tree-lined streets, while eyeing the shops and all the while secretly looking for Gabriella.

But the scent of food sends her over the edge today. Maddie managed to avoid eating breakfast that morning, carefully shuffling her food around her plate as Emily chattered about her wedding plans. Grateful when Ruth removed her plate before anyone noticed.

Ruth, as she still secretly thought of the family's maid.

Or was she a Domestic Helper?

Or servant?

The thought brings her back to the dream. The server standing over her, waiting for her order.

"Aren't you going to eat, Maddie?

Maddie jumps, looks over her shoulder, and sighs at the sight of her colleague from across the hall. Mary Ann poked her head into the office while Maddie was lost in thought.

"You usually go to the deli, right? Can I get you anything? I'm heading there now." Mary Ann's eyes shift to the clock.

"Oh, no. No, thank you. I'm really into this project and just," she taps a pile of folders on her desk, "I'll break for lunch later, really eager to finish."

"That's good for you," her voice saccharine. "It's good to know when to keep going. And when your time is up."

What the fuck?

"Excuse me?"

"When it's time to take a break. You know. Everything in perfect balance. It's the way we do things in Silver Spring." She tilts her head this time as if her exaggerated smile weighs heavily on her.

Maddie nods, returning her best expression of friendly agreement, secretly counting down the seconds until the woman leaves her alone again. Mary Ann heads down the hall, her heels clinking in the distance as she hums a familiar tune Maddie's grandmother used to like.

I Say a Little Prayer For You

Doesn't anyone here listen to FM?

But why would they? Maddie hasn't seen any sign of a radio since she's been here.

She forces the smell of tuna sandwich out of her mind. As for the cryptic words Mary Ann said…

She didn't say that. You heard wrong. You're tired.

Maddie pulls the folders closer to her. The stack almost reaches her chin. The assignment is to sift through the old files and find anything amusing or, what was the word Janice used? Aesthetic. Matching Silver Spring aesthetic for an event everyone has been buzzing about this week.

Silver Pride

At first, the name conjured images of rainbow flags and celebrations all through the month of June. That's what Pride meant where she was from. In another place. Another life.

The memory makes her think of Rae and all they will miss in this isolated place. No parades. No celebrations. Not even the gratuitous displays in department stores. Maddie doesn't know what Silver Pride is, but she knows what it isn't.

From what she has gleaned so far, the event commemorates the founding of the town. The residents have a parade, speeches and music, and some type of contest. The Counting. A harvest of some sort.

At first she through it would be like any number of June festivities celebrating Pride. But a brief conversation left her blushin gand corrected by her peers whose scolding glances were enough to make her feel chastened for her mistake.

The first few folders contain copies of photos from past Silver Pride days. Benign. Quaint. The stuff of small towns. A fire truck festooned with a wreath, smiling children holding ice cream cones. A row of couples dressed in formal attire, she wonders if they had a beauty pageant.

She leafs through the pages, careful not to damage them.

By now she can recognize familiar faces in the photos.

Emily and Mark.

And Arianna.

The Dead Fiancée…

Maddie squints, then opens her eyes wide, as if to reset her mind.

She turns the page over, not wanting to linger on the view of the deceased bride, even when her eyes were full of life and tragedy was the farthest thing from anyone's mind.

By the time she has sorted through most of the files, making a pile of keepers and a pile to return to the basement, the stacks before her are almost level with each other. The copied images are dated. There are fewer photos, and the outfits are dated, even for Silver Spring.

She turns over a photo of women standing around a tree, their hair concealed in bonnets. Next, a flimsy, thin paper is covered in handwritten notes. Maddie squints. This is unusual. She pulls the paper closer to read the fading words.

A ledger. Or sales note. It doesn't belong with the rest. Someone must have put it here accidentally.

The month is faded, but she can see the faded number twelve. And the year, 1943.

A note follows in penmanship she hasn't seen in at least a generation.

'The land heretofore chartered as Silver Spring and henceforth known as Silver Spring for all intents and purposes, shall extend on the southernly most border from Bass Creek. The easterlymost border, encompassing the lands formerly known as Sitterly Homestead. Westerly most to the border of Greenridge. Northern, extending to the border of Eagle Mountain.'

The names hardly ring a bell. Maddie keeps reading.

'Silver Spring is hereby established legally and rightfully surrendered each part and in full from the following:

Edgar Stetson and family and all future heirs.

Margaret Bloom and family and all future heirs.

Martin Freeman and family and all future heirs.

And any occupants past or present who have occupied in part or full, or at any time, any establishments within the borders of the township formerly known colloquially as Freemont and officially as...'

Maddie's eyes widen.

She's never been woke like Carolyn. But in her gut, she feels a jolt at the sight of the name. Her cheeks grow hot.

There, in black and white, a cancel-worthy slur with the word "town" attached, just as ordinary as if it read "Manhattan," or "Denver."

She turns the page over; a continued note is penned on the paper beneath this one.

'Having been given an opportunity to stake a legal claim to the town and having failed, all rights forthwith are surrendered to the following, fully and completely, and to their heirs and designees only.

Jeremiah Silver

Randolph Harris
Harriman Whiting
David Carrolton
Joshua Avery
Who on this day set forth a new settlement paid in full and legally owned. Silver Spring, New York.'

Maddie eyes the signatures of each of the founders.

Ralph Harris.

Randolph Harris.

She returns to the first page and reads the names again. The residents of Freemont.

Maddie scrambled through the papers, looking for any paperwork on these families. The previous residents. A bill of sale. A contract.

Having been given an opportunity to stake a claim… and having failed
…

Where were the receipts?

"Maddie," Janice's voice broke her concentration.

Damn. Is this really going to be the day everyone sneaks up on me?

She closes the folder, as if hiding a secret.

"Hi, um, how was lunch?" She winces, too late to retrieve the words. She feels her cheeks redden again.

Janice stops short, as if trying to remember what she ate.

"It was good. Thank you. I see you've really taken to planning for Silver Pride."

"Oh, it's fascinating. Yes," Maddie's voice is flat.

"That's nice. I trust you'll find it as fun as the rest of us."

"I'm sure I will," she nods.

"I'm heading out for an appointment," Janice begins, eyeing the stacks of folders. "Why don't you wrap up here and call it a day?" She smiles as if encouraging Maddie to play hooky.

"Oh, thank you. Sure. I'll just organize these so I can pick up where I left off."

"Sounds good. I'll lock the door, so you don't have to."

Janice is down the hall before Maddie returns to rifling through the files. But her sense of intrigue is dulled now. She doesn't want to know what else she may find. Not now. Not today.

As she walks home that night, Maddie replays the conversation with Janice. Something doesn't fit. Not her awkward question about lunch. Not the appointment.

Maddie stops in her tracks.

No one locks doors in Silver Spring.

CHAPTER 31

She ignored the dream all day, but now, tossing and turning on the unicorn bed, Maddie can't get the images out of her mind. When she can no longer pretend sleep is looming, Maddie sits up, her forehead tense and dry eyes craving darkness she refuse. The hollow feeling of exhaustion and indigo shadows on the walls tell her it must be after midnight but not yet dawn.

She sits on the edge of the bed, facing the dollhouse across from her. In the dark it is no longer a beautiful relic. Like a haunted doll, the child's toy now seems ominous. Slivers of light line the edges showing a cross-section of the model Victorian home, but shadows lurk deep in each room. She leans closer as if looking for clues. In the living room, a hutch stands on tiny wooden stilt legs, it's edges curved.

Her eyes drift to the tiny kitchen where miniature appliances sit frozen in time. In the back of her mind, she hears water gushing from the faucet, then sputtering.

"John," her mother calls in the memory, "Can you take a look at this?"

She sees her father stride into the room, humming an old song by a band called Chicago. He pauses, staring at the faucet then frowns and shakes his head.

"What is it?" Her mother asks in a pensive tone.

"It's what I was afraid of."

"Oh, God," she puts her hands on her hips. She opens her mouth again, perhaps to complain, but before she can speak, Maddie's father spins her into an embrace.

"It's a loooove emergency…." He begins in what she used to think of as a silly voice.

Her mother laughs, then catches sight of her watching from the living room.

"Not in front of Madison, behave, John."

The image fades into the dark room. Maddie tries to preserve it, but it's already dissipated. Her stomach sinks, the feeling of a rollercoaster dropping suddenly.

She falls back onto the bed again, rolls on her side, and falls asleep.

CHAPTER 32

She remained a distance behind Rae, remembering what Gabrielle, Gabriell-a, she corrects herself, said about cameras everywhere.

Rae is headed in the direction of the park.

She catches up with the girl midway down the block. Rae looks over their shoulder, face shifting from alarm to relief when they recognize who was behind approaching.

"Hey, we need to talk," Madison begins.

She falls in step beside the girl now and looks awkwardly around, trying to spot any eavesdroppers.

"So, I think I met someone," Maddie begins in a low tone.

Rae turns to meet her eyes, a wry grin on their face, "aw, you and David hit it off, did you? Well, that's great, and all this time we thought he didn't go to your church."

"What do you mean? My church? But, no, it's not David. That's not what I meant," Madison tries again. "I mean I spoke to someone, I think she may be like us, I mean like whatever it is we are, she's not like the rest of Silver Spring."

Rae's face is serious now. They glance at Maddie but then keeps walking, eyes on the ground..

Maddie continues, "Gabrielle," for safety, she thinks it's best to blend in for now, "Gabrielle, the woman who works with David, she's a historian, she does research, I guess? She said there are cameras everywhere in Silver Spring. Downtown at least, maybe in other places."

"Yeah, we know," Rae begins, "I mean no one knows exactly where they are, but the cameras have always been there. But they don't check the ones near our house," Rae seems confident about this.

"How do you know?"

"Because, my Grandma is one of the founders. She's more powerful than the mayor, in case you didn't notice. No one is going to spy on her."

"Okay, but there's something else. I think you know it. Something about Silver Spring. It's not like other small towns," Maddie begins.

Rae grimaces, they jab their cheeks with an index fingers, twisting their fingers in a mockery of dimple-faced innocence, "Of course, Silver Spring isn't like any other town. There's no crime and we all share values…"

They laugh, but Madison hears something strained edgy in their voice.

"Emily senses it. But she doesn't know it," Madison understands as she is saying it, "because she's never left town. But you have. You've broken through the… the whatever it is. You go against them. So, you understand it, and you must know, right? You must know there's something to the signs, the cameras, and rats, and the weird thing with the food at the restaurant," Maddie's heart wrenches she doesn't want to say these things about Silver Spring. Everyone has been so good to her. She thinks with remorse of the unicorn bed. Sees Emily's face glow with excitement as they shop for dresses, thinks of Billie Jo and Grandma Winnie. "I mean, don't get me wrong, I love it, it's home, it's beautiful and there's a lot that's good about it, but there are some things that are a little different. I guess it's like Amish, like a different culture, and it's different but it's not bad…"

"No," Rae stops her mid-sentence, her hand raised in disagreement. She shakes their head, "no, that's what you don't get. Different isn't allowed and it is bad."

They walk in silence for a few moments. Maddie begins again.

"You tried to tell me something. At Arianna's memorial. Do you remember?"

Rae grabs her arm. Maddie jumps, then stops in her tracks. She looks at the child who shifts her head slightly, gesturing to an area across the street. Maddie's heart freezes. She follows Rae's gaze and sees Grandma Winnie leaving a store with a paper bag in hand.

She's too far away to have heard them. Maddie is sure of it. But there is something sinister in Grandma Winnie's expression. She smiles, but her eyes are cold.

Dead.

CHAPTER 33

A week goes by before Maddie sees Rae alone. Seven evenings of tense dinners, eerily quiet and strained. *Or is it just me?* Maddie wonders.

In that time, every word from Emily has been about wedding dresses or venues, or cakes.

Rae had been conspicuously absent and Maddie overheard Grandma Winnie mention she was at "coaching" again.

Grandma Winnie's frame has become more gaunt. Maddie notices she has swapped out most of her meal for additional wine. She was slurring her words last night when she smiled at Emily and said, "Tomorrow the Bellingers are expecting you at their shop to try on wedding dresses."

Emily's face lit up, and she looked at Maddie.

"You'll come too, right? Please? I need you there to help me deal with Desirae."

Maddie nods.

"I haven't seen her around much. Is she okay?"

Billie Jo coughs, then forces down the portion of dinner she was chewing and wipes at her mouth with her napkin before taking a long sip of wine.

Grandma Winnie averts her eyes. Only Emily looks at her directly and answers.

"She's back in coaching," Emily rolls her eyes as she says this. "She's just incorrigible."

Incorrigible Bastard

The name from her dream resurfaces in Maddie's mind.

"Oh, well, teenagers. You know." Maddie tries to sound casual.

Emily freezes, fork midair. She furrows her brows waiting for further explanation.

"I mean, you know, sometimes adolescence can be…"

Grandma Winnie interrupts her.

"Adolescence is an important time." Her voice is clear now. She looks at the table, eyes stern. "It is a time when people discover who they are. And learn their purpose. And those who don't learn their purpose? They become drifters. Trouble."

She raises her glass to her lips. Its edges stained maroon, and drinks.

They finish dinner in silence.

CHAPTER 34

On her second trip to Malinda's Bridal Salon, Maddie's soft stubble from her DIY buzzcut has grown to brown hair that extends to her chin. She no longer has any illusions about the venue being the type of salon she and her mother used to go to before her father died.

And she's no longer looking forward to a day of trying on dresses, like the last time she was here, with Emily, preparing for Arianna's wedding.

This time, the quaint refurbished building looms ominously amidst other stores bustling with Saturday shoppers. Rae carelessly flings the door open, and Emily follows behind her sister, but Maddie hesitates. She holds the glass door open for a moment, bracing herself for some horror she expects to see inside.

But only the same cream and white leather couches meet her eyes. The tables adorned with flowers and pitchers of water. Rows of formal gowns and perky, smiling saleswomen darting in different directions, arms loaded with dresses to bring to the fitting room or return to the racks.

Maddie walks in and lets the door close behind her. She watches as Emily makes a beeline for the wedding gowns. Her friend seems entranced. She wonders if the Bride-to-Be has forgotten her and Desirae following behind.

"Emily! It's a pleasure to see you here today."

Maddie turns in the direction of the woman's voice and sees a middle-aged woman with blonde hair hanging from a high ponytail in whisps. She has a pen tucked behind one ear. Her teeth are impossibly white.

"Here to shop for the big day," Emily responds. She walks toward the woman and embraces her in a friendly hug. Maddie notices Rae, arms folded, looking bored.

The older woman keeps a hand on Emily's shoulder as she regards her, "You're looking as slim and gorgeous as ever. Been doing the Bride-to-Be diet?"

Maddie thinks this question is rude.

She then remembers the pizzeria and wonders what the Bride to Be diet consists of.

Definitely not the Bossy Wife, she hears Carolyn chime in from her subconscious. She stifles a laugh, covering her mouth with her hand, pretending to scratch at an imaginary itch on her face.

"Thank you. And yes, I've been watching my figure for the big day." Emily smiles.

It's the happiest she's looked all morning. Her eyes are alight, not vacant and obsessive the way she's been in recent days.

The older woman drops her hand and looks around, eyeing Rae with an air of disgust and her with indifference before returning her gaze to Emily.

"And where are your mother and Grandma Winnie today?"

The vacant look returns to Emily's eyes as she answers, "Grandma Winnie is a little under the weather. Mother stayed home to keep an eye on her."

The woman frowns.

"Oh, how sad. And it's a tradition to shop for the big day with one's mother." She stares off into space for a moment, then her face brightens. "But Grandma Winnie is quite a woman. All she does, and at her age, we should all be so lucky. I hope she feels better soon."

Emily nods.

After a bit more dull pleasantries the older woman, who Maddie hears Emily refer to as Mrs. Dunphy, walks them to the bridal gown section. She rushes Emily from one rack to another. Taking on the role of her surrogate mother, helping her distinguish among the many shades of white.

To her surprise, Maddie is bored.

She used to think of weddings as exciting. She loved the idea of trying on dresses and even of assisting the bride to find the perfect dress. But now, all she can see are mountains of tulle and satin, beads and sequins, lace, and little silk flowers. She follows idly behind Mrs. Dunphy, who leads with her arm wrapped around Emily's. The older woman chatters to Emily, a din Maddie no longer hears. Rae is somewhere in the landscape but she's lost track of the child.

The soft beat of the overhead music is getting to her. It throbs in her temples. For the first time, she hears the lyrics…

"And I promise to be a good wife

Such a good wife

We'll have the good life…

Just you and me…"

The words send chills up her spine.

She turns to her right and steps on something hard. Her heart leaps to her throat. On the floor beneath her foot is a creamy, smooth, disembodied arm.

She lets out a sigh realizing it belongs to a nearby mannequin. Maddie picks up the arm and leans it against the mannequin out of the way of foot traffic. When she looks up, icy plastic eyes stare down at her. The lifeless face reminds her of Emily.

Maddie watches, expecting the mannequin to blink. Breathing fast, she suddenly wants to leave. Sweat drips along her upper arms and down her neck.

She looks around but sees no one. Just the judgmental stares of mannequins in each corner. They wear lace and tulle and silk and even a feather boa. Their painted-on faces no longer vacant. Nor smiling.

They sneer.

Maddie turns away, looking for an opening in the aisles, a walkway out from this now too-crowded corner of the shop.

Salon.

But the racks of dresses seem to surround her.

No longer mountains of various shades of white, but an avalanche.

And I'll be a good wife

It's my promise to youuuu

The disembodied voice sings.

It's the right thing to doooo-oooo

She tries to call Emily's name but her voice is gone.

The room begins to spin.

Maddie feels sick, as if the dresses are encircling too close.

She can't breathe. The air is stale and suddenly smells like an old closet. Like mothballs and sweat.

To be a good wife for you-ooo-ooo

A hand comes down hard on her shoulder. Maddie spins around, expecting to stare up into the face of one of the mannequins.

But it's Rae.

"You okay?" the child asks.

Maddie blinks. The room is back to normal. The dresses are in rows. Not clustered around her. The mannequins have a blank impression of facial features, nothing more.

The suffocating closet smell is gone. Replaced by the floral scent of roses and the soft hints of citrus from the fruit infused jugs of water.

"I think I need some air."

"Be right back," Rae calls over her shoulder, walking her out of the store.

"What's going on?" Rae asks quietly when they are outside.

"Can we sit in the car a minute?"

Rae shrugs and they walk to the car together.

"I don't know what happened," Maddie began, breathing normally again. "I felt like I was suffocating, like the room suddenly got small and, like, the dresses were suffocating me."

Rae nods, half smiling, "Yep, that's about how I feel about marriage. Of course, that's why I get sent to coaching."

Maddie's eyes widen. "The coach isn't like, for grades?"

Rae laughs. "No. I can do fine in school when I want. No. In Silver Spring, if you don't dream of marrying a man, settling down, and being brainwashed, then you go to coaching. It's how they deal with people who don't conform."

She sounds angry now.

"What do they, um, do?" Maddie asks.

Rae looks toward the store, her eyes now distant. "They try harder to brainwash you. If that doesn't work, they do other things."

"And if that doesn't work?" Maddie ventures, wanting to know more but not daring to pry.

"You conform. You preserve the town's traditions," she says this in an imitation of Grandma Winnie's voice, "or you get stuck with two options."

"Which are?"

"You ever wonder how my family has a slave?"

Maddie is taken aback by the word.

"She's a maid, right? A helper? What's the word, a domestic…"

"Slave," Rae interrupts her. "She doesn't get paid. She doesn't have freedom. She lives in the basement."

Maddie's eyes widen. Her heart races. Rae only gives her a moment to consider this before continuing.

"Silver Spring is rich because the majority of workers… the gas station attendants, the restaurant staff, the janitors, the town's maintenance workers, they're all slaves."

Maddie's mouth drops open. She blinks, letting this sink in.

"But, the people I work with, we get a salary…"

"For now. So do the teachers. The doctors. The Upper Workers. But the Lower Workers aren't really workers."

They sit in silence for another moment.

"So, if you don't do well in coaching and you refuse to be a slave, what happens then?"

"They kill you, most likely, or you run away." Rae says this with no emotion. "But either way, they need to fill the void. So, they take a surrogate. A Fall Bride. That's why most people don't take those options."

Maddie is on the edge of her seat. A dozen questions ready to pour from her mouth when a knock on the window makes her jump.

She turns to see Emily, vacant stare replaced with a simmering anger.

She steps back so they can get out of the car.

"Desirae, really, did you have to start something today?" She glares at her younger sister.

"It was me, I was feeling lightheaded." Maddie chimes in quickly. "I must have been so excited this morning I skipped breakfast."

Emily's face softens. "Come back in, have some water. I'll see if Mrs. Dunphy has any snacks."

Maddie follows her as Rae trails behind them. Now more than ever, she dreads going back in and trying to maintain her composure among the rows of gowns.

The two remaining hours in the store pass in a slow procession of one rejected gown after another. Maddie, a hostage in the dressing room, feels her temples throb as the artificial lighting wears her down. She feels stifled under the watchful glances of Mrs. Dunphy who rushes to and from the dressing room with piles of satin, silk, and lace cascading over her shoulder.

Rae by her side has taken to biting her nails as if she, too, recognizes she is a prisoner surrounded by full-length lighted mirrors and closed doors rather than bars.

She glances at Rae in one of the mirrors, searching for some secret sign as if they could possibly continue their conversation through winks or tics and go unnoticed by the bride-to-be concealed in a stall before abandoning modesty and walking through the changing room in her underwear holding up one gown, rejecting another, and obsessing over details Maddie doesn't notice.

Rae's face is once again concealed behind a mask of teen angst and dismay. Set in a perpetual sneer that only irritates her sister more.

Maddie wants to ask so many questions but wills herself to remember where she is, as if she could forget. There is no clock. She reaches for her pocket for the first time in months only to remember she has not owned a cell phone for some time now. She's been so swept away in the appeal of Silver Spring, she barely noticed.

Emily asks her opinion of yet another gown that she can't decipher from the last five and Maddie forces herself to smile and perk up her voice.

"It looks beautiful on you. But then, they all do. It's whatever makes you happy."

"Nooo!" Emily whines, closing her eyes and nearly sinking to the floor. "It's not what makes me happy! It's what is perfect. It has to be perfect." She repeats the phrase as if possessed and then drops another gown to the ground in a heap.

Mrs. Dunphy leans down, Maddie hears the woman's knee creak. Sees her lift a hand reflexively to rub the tip of her knee as she hesitates for a moment before gathering the lace and pile of mis formed lace and beads and rises again to stand, her face smiling and friendly, and hurries from the room.

Is she one of them?

Did she refuse to conform?

Or is this her job?

How do you know the difference?

Emily steps into another gown. Maddie searches her memory for interactions, interrogating scene after scene for clues to this bizarre caste system.

"Don't pretend you don't know," a voice interrupts.

Maddie's head snaps up. There, in the dressing room, adorned from head to toe in the ornate bridal fashion, stands a figure, her face covered in a veil.

Maddie blinks.

I'm seeing things.

A familiar laugh taunts her.

Carolyn.

My blood sugar must be low.

"Girl, stop fooling yourself," Carolyn lifts the veil. Maddie forgot how radiant she is. She's the only woman she's ever met with such beauty. No makeup. All natural.

Carolyn smiles, walking toward her, ballooning white tulle shuffling with every step. "You've seen this before. Haven't you?"

Maddie is stunned. She can't think. Can't speak. Her mind blank.

Maddie's mouth is dry. She tries to swallow but can't.

"But you never liked having these talks. Like you didn't want to think the one who threw my ass out on the street would come for you, too."

Her heart races.

She opens her mouth to respond. Tries to form words.

Carolyn, you're wrong, she wants to say.

A million excuses line up in her throat but the words won't come out.

"That's how it works, hon. There's even a poem about it. When the obvious scapegoats are gone, the privileged ones are next."

Maddie closes her eyes, bile rising in her throat.

She lifts her hand to cover her mouth, willing herself not to vomit. When she opens her eyes, Carolyn is gone. Across from her is only her own reflection in the mirror.

"Maddie?" Rae's voice calls from somewhere behind her.

She can't answer, still confused about what just happened.

"Maddie?" Again, this time she feels Rae's hand on her shoulder.

She manages to turn, facing the child, whose eyes widen at the sight of her face.

"You look whiter than these dresses. Sit down." Rae guides her to a cream sofa and pours water from a jug on the table nearby.

Behind them, the dressing room door creaks open again. Emily emerges, twirling and turning, satin skirt decorated with pearls and beads sway with her elegant body.

"I think I found the one!" Emily's eyes are lit up with enthusiasm.

But not like Carolyn's. Emily isn't radiant. She's intense. Something in Maddie's mind makes her think the look is that of a predator. Ferocious.

"Thank God!" Rae claps their hands.

Maddie gulps water from the cup quickly and forces a "It's the best, definitely" hoping the unusually high octave of her voice doesn't give away her nerves.

Emily buys the dress and schedules an appointment to return for a final fitting. She leaves the Bridal Salon walking on air in contrast with Rae's clomping footsteps. Maddie trails behind them, a human train dragging on the dusty ground behind the bride in brilliant white.

When she reaches the parking lot, she breathes a sigh of relief and momentarily falls back, leaning her body against the exterior of the salon. She takes in the fresh air and sunlight, relieved it's over.

Her stomach growls and she heads toward the car again. Something to her right catches her eye. A movement in the periphery of her vision. A bird perhaps. She turns to follow the motion and her gaze lands on an oil spot on the ground.

Someone's car needs a check-up, she thinks.

But it isn't iridescent. It isn't black. It's red. And at the far end of the stain is a line that runs to a white hem lightly brushing the ground. She raises her eyes, ready to tell the bride to watch her gown and avoid the stain.

It's too late. Rust stains the skirt. She follows a drop of blood to the bodice of the dress, heart frozen. She can't look away. The arms framing the dress are tinged with blue and caked with dirt.

She doesn't want to look. Can't look away.

The last thing she sees before Emily calls her name, breaking her out of the trance, is the woman's hand, twisted, her finger crooked and beckoning, summoning Maddie. On the woman's head is a crown made of leaves the colors of blood and straw.

CHAPTER 35

Rae's voice sounds oddly concerned, "I think Maddie needs some food. She looked a little tired while we were in the Salon." But Emily doesn't look over her shoulder and Maddie thinks it's just as well. Let the bride-to-be remain distracted with wedding plans.

What's clear from their conversation on the ride home is that Emily saw no trace of the woman in orange, her gown streaked in blood.

The Fall Bride

But did Rae see? Or am I losing my mind?

She's used to hearing Carolyn's voice. With the exception of a few weeks since she first came to Silver Spring, Maddie heard her best friend's voice in a running conversation since their falling out.

She shivers recalling the episode in the dressing room. It wasn't a dream. It felt real. And it was the the first time Carolyn ever appeared in full apparition style. Even after the loss of her father, she could barely conjure an image so vivid of in her clearest memories.

Could Carolyn be dead?

Tears blur Maddie's vision. She wipes at her eyes, pushing the notion away. Hoping no one is looking.

It can't be that. Anything but that.

Can someone haunt you while they're still alive?

And what about the woman in the bloody dress?

Was she the Fall Bride from Jessica's drawing? And how did the child know about her?

She wants to talk to Gabriella. Her hand instinctively feels into her purse, where a phone would have been nestled in another life. She doesn't miss the constant distraction of cell phones, which no one seems to have in Silver Spring. But at times like this she misses having the ability to send a discreet text.

The questions she longs to ask will have to wait for tomorrow. She'll catch Gabriella after work. She doesn't know how long it will take to get to talk to Rae again with no one else around.

First, she has to try to sit through dinner. She dreads Billie Jo asking about their trip.

"It was exciting. First the dresses tried to suffocate me, then my friend's ghost appeared in the dressing room, even though she's still alive I think? And then a definite ghost who made me crash my car but also may be a real person caught me outside." She imagines herself answering.

But Billie Jo only has eyes for Emily at dinner and her fascination with every boring detail of dress shopping is a welcome diversion.

Maddie tries to focus on her food. Hypoglycemic or not, she should eat. But she's not hungry. She pushes rice pilaf and lamb around on her plate. Her appetite diminished more as she realizes a slave has been feeding her.

Maddie is so consumed by the dawning feeling of guilt, she almost doesn't notice the wet, red splatter that dots the tablecloth and her left hand at the same time.

She jumps in her seat, her breath catching.

"I'm sooo sooorry," Grandma Winnie leans toward her, wiping the liquid from her hand with her napkin. Her breath wafts close to Maddie's face and she realizes then it is not blood. Just red wine.

Grandma Winne's tone is different.

She's actually slurring her words.

She reaches a thin, elegant hand down to dab the drops of wine from the tablecloth, but only spreads the mess further. Grandma Winnie stretches across the table, reaching for the bottle of wine. Her daughter and son-in-law stare at her, eyes wide, too polite to confront her.

"Well," Grandma Winnie says, "can't let it go to waste. That's alcohol abuse," She pours a full glass, and a splash slips over the edge. This time, she lets it go.

She sips and then slurps, the portion she just filled.

"I think I'll have some as well. Pass the bottle, Emily" The girl's father interjects. Maddie has not seen him drink and suspects he is doing it to keep the bottle away from his now thoroughly sloshed mother-in-law.

Maddie observed Mark and Glen instructing the Harris women in tones that remind her of a 1950s sitcom that didn't age well. But tonight, Mark's tone is more aggressive. As if he's trying to resume control.

Maybe he's just worried.

It can't be good for someone her age to drink this much. Then again, if you've lived as long as Grandma Winnie, shouldn't you enjoy whatever you want?

"I know what you're trying to do, and I don't appreciate it," the elder matriarch points a finger at her son-in-law.

"No one is trying anything Mother, are we?" Billie Jo responds. "You're one of the founders of this town. If you want a drink, you have a drink. You've certainly earned it."

Billie Jo crosses her hands in front of her on the table. For a moment, Maddie is reminded of an old Saturday Night Live routine in which Dana Carvey played a zealous Church Lady.

"Oh," Grandma Winnie perks up in her seat. She turns her face slightly, eyes wide and mouth smirking. Maddie can't tell if she's agreeing or about to goad her daughter into an argument.

Her muscles tense.

"Oh, you want to talk about what I earned? Oh yes. My Legacy," Grandma Winnie's voice sarcastic. She exaggerates each word.

Maddie has heard of rich people using wills and inheritances to control their families. She braces herself, expecting this to become a battle of the proverbial wills.

But instead, Grandma Winnie lifts her glass, though empty, and tips it to her mouth before setting it back down.

"Let's talk about the legacy of Silver Spring. Shall we?"

"There is no reason to act like a child," Mark's tone authoritative, edging on condescending.

"Oh, no," she continues. "Let's talk about everything I've earned. Everything I've sacrificed." She's sitting up taller now. "All to get us to this day. When my Emily, my cherished Emily, is about to make us all proud."

Emily blushes and smiles ear to ear.

"And let's talk about my *other granddaughter*, shall we?" She turns to Rae.

"Mom, there's no need to…"

"Oh, there's no need is there? How much blood," she pounds her fist on the table on the word blood and Maddie jumps again, "has gone into making this town what it is. And for what? Oh, we're all just lucky your grandfather never lived to see the day."

"Mother, I think maybe you're tired," Billie Jo begins to rise from her chair.

"Oh, I'm tired all right. Tired of it all." She turns to Maddie, looking down at her. Maddie sits like a rabbit facing a hungry wolf, she expects some kind of reprimand. "Do you know," Grandma Winnie begins, "that this town was founded to be different? A safe haven. That was the intention."

"Mother, please"

"But you know what they say about the road to Hell. It's paved with good intentions." She looks down at Maddie, "Don't go looking for the Silver Spring. It's just a waste of your time dear."

"Mother, you're not well…"

"And the road to Silver Spring is paved with blood."

"Enough! You're drunk," Mark begins again.

Maddie sneaks a fast glance at Rae who is watching the scene unfold with a look of fear and curiosity.

"Mother, please, you're embarrassing yourself," Billie Jo walks toward her mother, making her way slowly around the table, trying to remain calm, but her tone is less patient now.

"Well maybe I should be embarrassed," she puts her hands to her hips, now fully standing, swaying from drunkenness. She drops one hand to the back of her chair to steady herself before resuming her indignant position. "After all, what's going to happen to my own blood? I'm forced to now spill my own blood? It won't be a secret then, dear. The rest of the world knows it."

Billie Jo is now standing over Maddie. She grabs her mother's upper arms firmly and pulls the older woman close to her, mimicking a gesture of affection. She walks her from the table.

"Come on, Mother. It's time for you to get some rest."

"Oh, sure, put me to sleep like a dog, why don't you. You know it's the truth."

Grandma Winnie continues ranting as Billie Jo walks her down the hallway to her room. Maddie can no longer understand what she's saying.

She lowers her eyes and waits for someone to say something. No one does. In silence, they continue eating. All except her, and Rae.

CHAPTER 36

Maddie wakes to a late morning sun reflecting warm tones on the walls of the unicorn bedroom. She blinks, remembers it is Sunday and she has nowhere important to go, and rolls on her side, covering her eyes with her arm and hoping for more sleep.

Outside, the sounds of Silver Spring fade in and out of her awareness. Even with her eyes closed, she can see the tree-lined street outside. The wraparound porches, Tudor homes, and Adirondack chairs. The sounds of distant lawnmowers, children laughing, and an occasional bird blend and harmonize, lulling her back to sleep. Her mind drifts into stillness for a moment before the jarring sound discordant from all the others causes her eyes to spring open again.

She tries to ignore the piano at first. But the notes march like soldiers on a fatal mission, a minor key that invades her ears, clashing with the pleasant sounds of suburbia.

She rubs her eyes and pulls herself up. May as well start the day.

And if Emily is playing the piano again, is that really such a bad thing? Her chest tightens as she recalls the last time, she heard Emily play the piano.

Arianna's wedding.

She covers her eyes with both hands and shakes away the images of that day.

Who can blame Emily if she wants to play dirges?

One song fades into another and as Maddie freshens up and heads for the stairs the tempo quickens to a frantic rhythm.

Emily often played old music, but Maddie recalls it was usually showtunes or oldies like the Beatles. Maddie's feet hit the landing; her footfalls disguised by the music. She feels it louder as if Emily is condemning the piano for its sins.

Maddie's no musician, but she winces, noting the timing is off. Disjointed, echoing in the hallway. She imagines the keys being struck with mallets instead of Emily's graceful fingers.

And then it stops.

Maddie leans through the threshold.

"Emily? It's great to hear you play-"

Disheveled white hair was not what she expected to see. Maddie is taken aback at the sight of the petite figure seated on the piano bench, fingers hovering just above the keys.

Grandma Winnie takes her time responding. She doesn't turn to face Maddie.

"Grandma Winnie?" she tries again.

The old woman doesn't move. Maddie approaches in the manner she would use if addressing a suspicious dog who may be friendly, or rabid. She regrets saying anything. If she hadn't spoken up, she could just slip out of the room, and tiptoe back upstairs.

Without turning to face her, the old woman speaks.

"That day is coming."

Maddie blinks. "What day? You mean Emily's wedding?"

No, you idiot. Why would she mean that? Maddie chastises herself. But can't think of any other events approaching.

Grandma Winnie shakes her head. She grunts a brief laugh. Maddie steals a glance at the clock in the dining room. Ten thirty in the morning. If Grandma Winnie is already drunk, it's a new record.

"We tried so hard." Grandma Winnie rises from the piano bench. She leans against the side of the instrument and slowly turns to face Maddie. Her movements are stiff. Her face pained. And something else. Tears? Her eyes glisten. They are bloodshot, but Maddie doesn't smell alcohol.

"I know. You're one of the founding families. You worked really hard to make Silver Spring what it is." Maddie tries to sound encouraging but it sounds patronizing.

Grandma Winnie's eyes are tired. The lines on her face seem deep, each accentuating some angst that is as foreign to her as that carried by Rae. It occurs to her how much the girl looks like her grandmother in this moment.

"And what is it?" Grandma Winnie looks past Maddie, as if she's asking the wall. Or a ghost. "What is Silver Spring?"

Maddie's mouth goes dry. She knows how she would have answered that question a month ago. But she doesn't know how to answer it now.

"It's, um, a nice, quiet, um, you don't lock your doors…" she stumbles. Each word a hollow betrayal. She can imagine Gabriella in her mind. And Carolyn.

"Nice and quiet." Grandma Winnie motions with her fingers, mocking, as if conducting an orchestra. "You know what isn't quiet?"

The song you were playing just now, Maddie wants to say, but she shakes her head instead.

"The graves aren't quiet." Grandma Winnie walks past her, looking at the family photos hung on the wall. Maddie follows her, trying to make sense out of the riddles.

"Are you missing your husband?" She offers.

"Nothing to miss. I see him all the time. In my nightmares. Just like all the others." Grandma Winnie's voice flat. "You can't escape your past."

Maddie freezes. The hairs on her neck stand on end.

She knows.

What will she do?

Has she told anyone?

"It just follows you. And it infects your future."

She tells herself the old woman said *effects*. But in her mind, Grandma Winnie's voice corrects her.

Infects.

Maddie imagines an illness spreading. Scenes flash through her mind. Rats scurrying at her feet at the Christmas party. Arianna's memorial, the bridal shop.

Her skin prickles. Maddie looks to her arms, expecting to see a rash, but all she sees are tiny goosebumps slowly perking along her arms.

Grandma Winnie's voice distracts her.

"Arianna was a good girl. As good as any girl in Silver Spring could be. She didn't deserve to be taken."

"Taken?" Maddie asks. No one ever specified what happened to Arianna. Was she abducted? Or murdered? Was it a suicide? An overdose?

"But no, no we don't lock our doors."

Grandma Winnie's mocking tone makes Maddie want to turn, run from the room, not look back. But her feet are frozen in place. Maddie tries to speak but her throat is dry. Her voice emerges in a high squeak. Like the rats. She closes her mouth and tries to generate saliva. She feels like choking. Her mouth is sandpaper.

"We don't lock our doors. We never had to lock our doors. But they did. And even then, they couldn't hide."

"Who? What do you mean?" Maddie finally forces the words.

Grandma Winnie faces the photos on the wall. Maddie isn't sure the woman is in a conversation with her.

"All this. Preservation. Our way of life. Our history."

Maddie puts a hand on the older woman's arm. She's cold. Maddie grasps the older woman's hand, frail and icy. Colder than the air in the room. Maddie

"Careful what you try to preserve. It all comes at a cost."

"Okay?" Maddie agrees still not understanding what the old woman is talking about but not wanting to sound rude.

"Can I make you some tea or coffee, Grandma Winnie?" She offers.

The old woman doesn't respond. Her eyes are vacant.

"Do you want to talk about it?"

God, not like that, you sound like a television therapist, Maddie tells herself. She doesn't know what else to do.

"None of them will tell you. You won't find it in the archives. What happened in the park. What happens. To maintain order. Keep it nice. Quiet. But I was there. For each one. God have mercy." Her voice drops to just above a whisper.

"God have mercy," she repeats. "For generations we had the best of everything. But what we did to get it…"

"Your hands are cold, Grandma Winnie, do you need to warm up? Maybe a rest?"

"I'll be hot in Hell." Grandma Winnie mumbles, but she lets Maddie walk her to the recliner and wrap her in a blanket. Maddie doesn't bother responding. She doesn't really want an explanation. The old woman is tired. Cranky. Maybe she's crazy.

Or maybe she's not.

But Maddie doesn't want to ask.

She doesn't want to know.

Grandma Winnie closes her eyes.

"It.. was… Lynch. There."

She must be sleepy.

How often did she hear her mother mumble gibberish as she drifted off to sleep?

Whoever Mr. or Mrs. Lynch was this was the first Maddie heard of them. But she didn't know everyone.

Grandma Winnie is snoring softly within minutes, and Maddie slips out the door and heads toward the park.

CHAPTER 37

Maddie studies the face of Randolph, Ralph, Harris frozen in time at the park. One among many busts of the founders. Stone eyes betray no sign of the man he was. She searches his face for a clue. A sign of deception.

It must be an honest mistake. Grandma Winnie's family has been so generous. So welcoming.

To you, Carolyn's voice emerges for the first time since the dream. It can't be like that.

Not the Harrises. Maddie walks along the flower lined path, reviewing the names of the other founders. Whose idea was it?

She stares scrutinizing the etched bearded grin of Jeremiah Silver. He must have been in charge. The town is named for him. Or was it Joshua Avery? She thinks she sees a glint in his eye. But his eyes are vacant. Empty.

You never believed. Carolyn speaks from her memory.

Maddie closes her eyes. Tears burn behind her eyelids.

"You never believed me when I told you this woman was no good!" Carolyn paces the living room in their apartment. Arms folded over her chest, hands rubbing nervously at her upper arms. She can't look Madison in the eyes. Carolyn turns away from her, leaning over the table, reading the letter again.

"I always had your back, Madison."

Her best friend's voice breaks.

"Always. And I needed you to stick with us on this. To stick with me on this."

"She's not the person you say she is," Madison tries, but her voice sounds weak.

Carolyn spins to face her, eyes red with tears, wide with panic.

"No, Madison. She is. And here is the proof. She's throwing me out."

"You should have just made a deal with her…" Madison tries to reason with her friend. The landlady was always accommodating. There was no need to call code and make demands. What did Carolyn expect?

"Madison, we have a deal. It's called a lease. She is supposed to do her end of the deal. That means dealing with the rats. The roaches. The broken stove. No hot water for two months, that's her side of the deal. We agreed to the plan, and you didn't even try."

Madison sniffles loudly. Tears escape her eyes. She breathes deep, palms covering her face. Pushes the scene away.

Like everything else before Silver Spring.

It can't be true.

She thinks of the Harrises sharing dinner. Welcoming her into their perfect home. Giving her the perfect life.

"It's a perfect day."

It takes Maddie a moment to recognize David's voice.

He hadn't sneaked up on her. She turns to find him still several feet away, waving.

She clears her throat.

"David, hello. How are you?"

"I haven't seen you since…" He lets the statement hang in the air.

She casts her eyes to the ground.

"I'm sorry. I just got overwhelmed at work and things have been so busy and…"

He leans close to her. She braces herself for a kiss. Even opens her mouth slightly. He brings his mouth to her ear and whispers.

"I know about you."

She freezes.

"Don't worry," he continues. "Your secret's safe with me."

"I don't know what you mean."

She lies. Partially. She really doesn't know what he means, exactly. But she thinks she does.

But there are cameras. Everywhere. They can't speak openly.

"We'll talk more. Soon," he continues. Then hugs her. She thinks it's for show. To cover himself.

"It's good running into you here." He says in his normal voice.

"Yes," she replies, still dazed.

"We'll have to get together sometime soon. Very soon. Perhaps with Gabrielle."

He holds her gaze a moment too long as he says this.

He knows.

"I haven't seen her," Maddie begins. But David is already retreating.

"You will," he replies, before waving again and walking away.

CHAPTER 38

Maddie took her usual place at the dinner table. Emily, Glen, Mark, and Billie Jo were already seated and talking about some town tradition Maddie could only glean pieces of from conversation.

The chair next to her, where Grandma Winnie usually sits, is empty. Not wanting to interrupt, she keeps her eyes on the empty placemat before her.

The servant, Ruth, enters, arms loaded with trays. Maddie smells baked ham, scalloped potatoes, and roasted vegetables. Her senses are affirmed as Ruth sets one steaming dish after another on the table.

"Thank you," Maddie says.

"Now Maddie, really," Billie Jo begins as Ruth rushes back into the kitchen, "like we've said before, you don't need to thank the help. It is their duty."

"Sorry, I forgot," Maddie casts her eyes down. She didn't want to apologize. She wants to take it back. To say Billie Jo is being unreasonable and bitchy. But she doesn't.

In the silence that follows, she realizes Rae would usually be the one to challenge her mother's authority. Maddie looks across the room at the space beside Emily.

Rae's seat is empty.

Maddie opens her mouth to ask about the child, but a crash distracts her.

"Christ on a cracker!"

Grandma Winnie's voice comes from the living room. Her words slurred. Maddie starts to rise from her seat, but Mark is already striding toward the direction of the noise.

"Grandma Winnie," he begins in a stern, yet patronizing voice.

"Oh? Is it Gramma Winnie?" she answers.

Grandma Winnie enters the room, staggering, holding herself up by the backs of chairs. In the distance, Mark places a now broken lamp on the shelf behind the table, presumably to be dealt with another time.

"Grandma Winnie," Billie Jo sounds impatient, rising from her seat as the older woman sinks into hers, "what have you done? You've broken a lamp. And you're drunk!"

Grandma Winnie looks proud of herself. "Broke a lamp, did I? Poor little lamp. Was it the one that Mary had?"

She lifts her fork and as if conducting an orchestra, begins singing Mary Had a Little Lamp.

"Enough, Grandma Winnie, you're making a scene!" Billie Jo takes the fork from the old woman's hand, almost jabbing Maddie's head in the process.

"I'll make a scene if I want to," Grandma Winnie spits back. "It's my house. It's my town. And this time, it's my granddaughter."

Billie Jo's face darkens.

"That's. Enough." She pronounces each syllable as if scolding a child.

Maddie glances around the table. Emily looks down at her plate, her lip twitching. Glen puts a hand over hers.

"If you can't compose yourself, I will remove you from the table." Billie Jo continues.

"You and what army?"

"Grandma Winnie," Mark stands over the older woman, his voice patronizing, "Remember what Dr. Needham said. Did you forget your medicine again?"

"Who needs medicine when you're shitfaced drunk?" Grandma Winnie reaches for a bottle of wine on the table, but Mark grabs it before she can. He places it down harder than intended in front of Glen.

"You forget yourself, Grandma Winnie," Billie Jo tries again in a saccharine voice. "And you forget we have company," she emphasizes the word as if it is giving some sort of clue.

"I forget nothing. I wish I could forget. But your husband has stolen my wine."

"Grandma Winnie," Billie Joe tries again, but the old woman interrupts her.

"Yes. Grandma. That means old. Old enough to know better. And old enough to not give a flying fuck."

Glen's face turns red, his mouth twists awkwardly as if he's trying not to laugh. Emily nudges him with her elbow.

"Sorry, dear," he mouths, averting his eyes.

Grandma Winnie ignores their exchange. She continues her speech, "I'm old enough to remember when this place was founded, and how…"

"Enough!" Billie Jo starts to pull the older woman from her seat by her arms. Maddie wants to intervene, to stop her, but she's frozen in place.

"And I can't forget. I see their faces every night. And soon it will be Desirae," she points a finger at Billie Jo, whose face is now close to hers, "and then it will be on your head. And we'll see how well you sleep at night. We'll see what Dr. Needham has to say about you when,"

"Okay, Grandma Winnie," Mark stands behind her, pulling the chair from the table, guiding his wife away from the elderly woman in the process. "Grandma Winnie, it's time for a nap. I'll get your pills."

"Stick them up your ass. You don't want to hear the truth. At my age, I've earned the right to drink. I've earned the right to say what I wanna say and if I wanna break a lamp, it's my fucking lamp…"

Ruth returns with a hypodermic needle and hands it to Billie Jo, who jabs the side of Grandma Winnie's shoulder. The elderly woman never saw it coming. She screams, swatting Billie Jo away, almost stabbing her palm with the needle in the process.

"Kill me if you want, I'm old. I buried Arianna. I buried how many other children? I won't bury my own granddaughter," she's hysterical now, "I did it. I did it. Ralph, and me, and all of you. Guilty, guilty …" her voice fades, and as she passes out in her chair, the last thing Maddie hears her say is, "from the time we hung that man…"

CHAPTER 39

Maddie wants to ask Grandma Winnie about the things she said. Billie Jo and Emily spend most of the prior evening convincing Glen and Maddie that the old woman's outburst was a product of drunkenness and senility. But Maddie suspected otherwise.

Glen smiled, poured a glass of wine for himself and Emily, and acted like it was any other visit. Maddie couldn't wait to leave the table. Later that evening, she lingered in the bathroom, leaning too close to the door. She caught bits of conversation between Mark and Billie Jo.

Something about Grandma Winnie always following tradition, this from Billie Jo. Followed by Mark in a softer voice, too low to hear clearly, in a tone of placating. She heard Rae's name mentioned but little else.

Maddie walks down the stairs bracing herself for the next landmine. She imagines Grandma Winnie waking up from whatever medicine she had been given and being in rare form and ready to go to battle again. She wants to talk to her alone before any more confrontations.

But the house is peaceful. Emily sits on the sofa, sipping tea and reading a book.

"Where is everyone?" Maddie asks, trying to sound casual.

Emily looks up, smiles, and nods toward the window, "Mom and dad went to a meeting of the town Austerity Committee and Glen had to put some extra time in at the office," she curves her hand in front of her mouth as if keeping a secret and pretends to whisper, "so he can afford some extra wedding expenses."

She giggles.

Maddie forces a smile. "The big day is almost here. Time flies."

"One month, ten days, five hours, but who's counting?" Emily jokes.

Maddie pushes her mouth into a wider grimace. Inside she's cringing. But Emily returns her gaze to her book, and Maddie takes the opportunity to slip out of the room and down the hall.

She stops outside Grandma Winnie's room, considering how to best approach the woman, before deciding to be direct. She knocks softly. Nothing. Again, slightly louder.

"Grandma Winnie?"

Nothing.

She doesn't want to be intrusive but maybe Grandma Winnie doesn't hear well? Was she wearing hearing aids? Maddie opens the door, blurting out the words as she does.

"Sorry, I just want you to know I believe…."

Silence.

A bitter taste burns up the back of Maddie's throat.

The older woman's quilted bedspread is made up perfectly. The surface of her dresser adorned with ornate perfume bottles shaped like tiny clowns and turtles and a train engine. A stuffed bear holds a heart beside an antique looking doll. A perfectly cleaned comb beside a wooden jewelry box.

The rocking chair holds a folded knit Afghan. At the foot of the bed, two fuzzy slippers, a perfect pair side by side.

The feet that should fill them float midair. Toes curled and blue. Maddie doesn't want to keep looking. She can't look away. Her eyes drift up against her will. The lavender nightgown. Pale hands dangle at her sides.

Before she can see the woman's lifeless face staring down at her from where her body hangs from the ceiling, Maddie is retching. She falls to the floor, her hands outstretched on the fluffy beige carpet.

Sinking to the ground like a sunflower. Cut down. Screaming. Inhaling the fumes from the puddle of vomit that desecrated the perfect bedroom.

* * *

Later that night, when the family is busy at the hospital making final arrangements, Maddie sneaks into Grandma Winnie's room again. She tells herself she needs to clean the vomit stain, although it has been gone for hours.

She lingers in the still room. Surveying again as if looking for clues. The doll regards her silently. Nothing is disturbed among the trinkets that marked the woman's life. Her possessions immaculate.

In a stupor of disbelief and desperation and numbness, Maddie wanders around the room. She eyes the framed photographs. She recognizes the picture of Ralph Harris from photos at the Preservation Society.

The nightstand holds a lamp, a Bible, and reading glasses. Maddie kneels on the floor, running her hands over the carpet where she vomited earlier. The carpet is clean. This ritual serves no purpose, and she knows it. She begins pushing herself back to her feet when something under the bed catches her eye. A box. Or a book. She slides a hand under the quilted bedspread and retrieves a box. It's light for its size.

Don't do it. Don't snoop. Let the woman rest in peace…

She tells herself as she opens the cover. Inside, a notebook. It's old and spiral bound. Perfect penmanship marks the pages. Maddie flips through pages of dates, names, and notes that mean nothing to her.

Put it back.

She ignores herself.

The notebook is thick. As she flips through, the writing changes. No longer a ledger, the pages contain journal entries.

July 15, 1968, September 29, 1984, August 14, 1992…

She picks a date and reads.

July 29, 1996- Preparation for the "Festival." This year, the Surrogates are Danielle Martin, Jennifer Needham, Dolores Pellman, Janus DeMarco- from away.

Shame, Jennifer Needham had promise. Good family. Pure Blood.

She flips to another page.

August 20, 1999

Several children went missing. Believed to be taken by people from away. Must be more careful. Surrogates- Maya Horne. This can't continue.

Maddie flips to the end of the notebook to read Grandma Winnie's most recent entries. Her heart pounds as she turns the pages. But when she hears the car pull into the driveway, she shoves the book back into the box, then removes it again, replacing the box.

A car door slams.

Maddie runs down the hall as the second car door shuts.

She is up the stairs by the time she hears Emily's voice and another car door closing, the sound muffled from a distance.

By the time what is left of the Harris family enters the house without their matriarch, Maddie is back in Emily's room. Heart pounding, a buzzing sound in her ears, she scans the room for a place to hide the ledger.

Bookshelf filled with old paperbacks. Too obvious.

Behind the bulletin board, not secure enough.

She turns to the table by the bed, placing the ledger in her mouth, careful not to taste it. Maddie gently lifts the wooden doll house, careful not to rattle the delicate furniture as she does. Maddie feels beneath it. There is a ridge along the bottom edges, a space before the floor. She sets the dollhouse back down, then lifts the front just enough to slide the ledger underneath.

CHAPTER 40

The funeral notice in the paper invited the people of Silver Spring to pay respects to Winnifred Harris, last of the founders, who died peacefully at home of old age. Maddie recalls the way Mark and Billie Jo went about their business, faces blank, after discovering the corpse hanging from the ceiling of the old woman's bedroom.

Now, sitting in the backseat of Mark's car as the Harris's drive to the funeral home, Maddie leans into the car's seat, quieting her breath. Making herself invisible as they pass the quiet sidewalks. Beside her, Emily stares out the window, silent. In the driver's seat, Billie Jo speaks occasionally to Emily or Mark in a pressured tone. They ignore Maddie, and it's just as well.

Still no sign of Rae.

The funeral home is a brick building tucked behind the church and hidden from view by a row of trees. The first guests arrived early, crowding the receiving line. Maddie slips toward the back of the room. On an oak table, a young Winnifred, not yet a teen and far from her grandmother years, smiles in black and white prints. Her eyes are deep and thoughtful. Beside this photo, another. Winnifred as a young woman, arm in arm with Randolph Harris. Wedding veil spilling down her shoulders. Face beaming with pride. Randolph's face reserved, yet kind. In the third, the departed woman is one of many standing before a tree. Maddie recognizes the park. Grandma Winnie still not yet middle-aged and just Winnie then, or Winnifred. She and Randolph stand in the middle of a phalanx of faces.

They seem proud. Jovial. Like they just won a contest. Perhaps it's a picnic. Or a summer holiday festival.

Maddie shifts her gaze from one photo to the other, trying to reconcile the woman who looked so innocent, who had been kind to her, with what she had recently discovered.

Grandma Winnie, and her husband, helped found a place she felt safe and at home by driving away others who were there first. And wasn't that the story of America? Maddie wasn't woke like Carolyn, but she wasn't naïve.

Young Winnifred, full of life. Winnifred the bride. Winnifred, the Founder. The grandmother. The photos fade, replaced by the image of Grandma Winnie laughing at dinner. Welcoming her to the family.

Grandma Winnie, her finger crooked, chastising Rae to go upstairs and put on her shoes. Forcing her grandchild back into a box so suffocating it could be a coffin.

Grandma Winnie, drunk, raising her voice defiantly to Billie Jo a few nights ago.

Grandma Winnie ranting about the things that haunt her. Rising from the piano, eyes brimming with dry despair before murmuring to herself as she fell asleep.

Maddie lifts the picture of Grandma Winnie surrounded by townspeople, standing before an oak. Tree limbs stretch to form a sprawling canopy.

"Be careful what you try to preserve…it comes at a cost." Grandma Winnie's voice whispers from the recesses of Maddie's mind.

In the photo, the young matriarch smiles. Her chin out, eyes bright.

Maddie has so many questions.

"You won't find it in the archives."

Hints of sunlight shine through the tree limbs in the photo.

"What happened in the park. What happens. Every so often."

Maddie's eyes drift to the top of the tree, leaves shimmering what must have been warm harvest light.

"To maintain order. Keep it nice, as you said. Quiet. But I was there."
Some of the townspeople in the photo stand with arms folded, as if accomplishing some chore.
"I was there for each one. God have mercy."
And Grandma Winnie, dead center.
"For generations we had the best of everything."
The townspeople all in their Sunday best.
"But what we did to get it…"
Something catches Maddie's eye.
"I'll be hot in Hell."
She recalls Grandma Winnie's words.
Her eyes focus.
Silver.
No, metal.
She knows what it is.
Leaning against the tree.
Maddie hears Grandma Winnie mumble the word. Not a name.
Maddie's eyes dart from the tree. To the ladder. To the smiling white faces.
Something is missing. Removed before they snapped the photo.
They removed the body Maddie now understands. They removed the rope. But no one bothered to remove the ladder.
Grandma Winnie, her eyes glinting with joy.
Suddenly repulsed as if the object is a snake poised to strike, Maddie jumps back, dropping the picture. Glass from the frame shattering.
Around her, silence falls over the din of mourners paying their respects. Her back is to the crowd, but she feels eyes burning into her. She can't move.
Two hands gently cover her shoulders.
A voice whispers, close to her ear.
"Maddie, it's okay. Let's go for a walk."
Maddie is relieved to hear David's voice. Without looking back, she allows herself to be escorted from the room.

CHAPTER 41

Maddie is relieved to hear David's voice. To feel is hands on her shoulders, guiding her from the crowded funeral home where it seems all eyes are suddenly on her. She drops her eyes, examining rows of shoes, not wanting to see the bodies, faces, looks of shock and disgust. Her world becomes a tunnel wide enough to contain only the path in front of her. The maroon carpeting with gold trim. Then the heavy wooden door, the hallway, three steps, and then in the fresh air she can breathe.

David puts an arm around her shoulders. His gesture of affection stiff yet comforting. He's the only one who came to her aid. The one.

The one.

One, her mind plays on the word.

One of them.

Maddie jerks away from David, nearly knocking him off balance. His eyes widen and he lifts both hands as if trying to back away from a rabid animal.

"It's okay, you're okay," he begins.

"No, I'm not. And neither is this place, and neither are you," Maddie raises her voice.

David's face no longer surprised, but pale and alarmed.

"We're going to talk about it, I promise," He begins slowly, in his best hostage negotiator voice, "but not here. Just wait. Come with me."

Maddie searches his face for some sign he understands. But how could he? He's from here. This is normal to him. She looks around desperately, seeking a familiar face. Gabriella. Rae. For a moment she expects to see Carolyn walking down the street.

The streets are empty, of course. Because everyone is inside the funeral home paying tribute to Granda Winnie. Everyone except her and David.

And Gabriella, and Rae, who have been conspicuously absent.

She eyes David suspiciously, sizing him up. What's the worst that could happen if she follows him? His arms are not particularly muscular. He's not scrawny but doesn't seem exceptionally strong. She doubts anyone in Silver carries guns.

Seeing no better option, she walks toward David, lets him stiffly hold her hand and guides her toward a side street she recognizes.

The in-law house where she spoke candidly with Gabriella. Will she be there?

Her question is answered wordlessly by the emptiness inside the small house. David opens the door, standing back to allow Maddie to enter first.

Wasn't the door locked?

Maddie hadn't noticed if he used a key to get in.

"Where's Gabriella?" Maddie turns to him, eyes piercing, an accusation in her voice. Intentionally pronouncing the 'a' at the end of the young woman's name erased by residents of Silver Spring.

He doesn't flinch.

"She's fine. She's working on a project." David's delivery is patronizing. Slow, as if she's a child on the verge of a tantrum.

He continues.

"I can cover for you. A little. But it will only go so far," he begins. But Maddie cuts him off, arms crossed over her chest.

"Cover for what? I didn't do anything. This place is fucked-"

"Please, you must listen," David holds his hands up. He looks around as if frightened someone may hear. But everyone is at the wake. At least that's what she assumes. Still, she lowers her voice.

"Cover for what?"

"People are going to talk. They're already talking about…"

She starts to interrupt him. To tell him she doesn't care what people talk about, but he holds up a hand in a halting gesture and she lets him continue.

"We don't get outsiders here much. And when we do, they're, "he pauses considering his words carefully, "not always encouraged to stay. But you're an exception. They wanted you. The town wanted you."

"You're not making any sense. What are you talking about?"

"The Harrises welcomed you into their home because they had plans for you. And you seemed to be going with it but now, people are noticing things. They're starting to talk about whether you can be trusted. I can cover for you. I can chalk some things up to you not being from around here. But you've got to keep a low profile. What happened today, and at the council meeting, these things are giving you the kind of attention you don't want from very powerful people."

Maddie can't help laughing at the last statement. She squints in a look of disbelief.

"Powerful people? Here?"

"I'll try to explain but please, let's just sit and talk. You need to be calm for this. Please," David gestures to a worn chair and Maddie sits, still eyeing him warily. He joins her, sitting in a folding chair that looks unstable let alone uncomfortable.

David looks her in the eyes. She can sense he's uncomfortable. Like a parent forced to have 'the talk' with a child because they found a condom but not really looking forward to the task.

"I know what you saw in the picture. Most people here wouldn't notice it. Or if they did, they wouldn't react the way you did because they…." He pauses, looking over her head as if waiting for the words to be delivered from on high, "because they were never taught to react with anything but indifference."

"What about you?" Maddie is still guarded. She stares coldly at him.

"I had to learn. As a historian. And as someone who takes an interest in outsiders when they arrive. I didn't know the difference. But I learned."

"But you act just like the rest of them," Maddie begins.

"To survive." His eyes are wide and somber. "And I want you to survive. Because here is the thing you probably haven't put together. You will be given a choice. And you won't like either option. But your best bet for survival is to blend in."

"I don't want to blend in," she spits the last two words with contempt.

David sits back and folds his arms now, his turn to look skeptical.

"Oh, you don't? You fooled everyone here so far. You've passed all the tests. That's why they've taken you in. Allowed you to be part of the community."

Maddie feels the temperature in the room drop. Her mouth dries. She wants to speak but fears she will choke.

"A job at the Preservation Society?" David begins counting on his fingers, beginning with his thumb.

"Volunteering with kids at the library," he extends his index finger. Strike two.

"An invitation to Arianna's wedding," his count continues.

Maddie's eyes burn. She wants to be angry. To lash out. Accuse him of reading too much into her adaptation to the town. To insist she was just being polite and that when in Rome…

"You've blended right in at the Harris's. And when you saw things you didn't agree with, you didn't rock the boat. Your boss trusted you with documentation from the archives, so we know you know, and you didn't say a word."

She wants to cry and swallows hard, choking back tears.

"What was I supposed to do? I don't have my phone; I don't have my car…"

"You've had your car for months." David corrects her, no judgment in his voice.

Maddie feels the room close in around her. She recalls walking up the street after talking to Gabriella. Her car was in the driveway. Repaired, restored, and all but forgotten. How long ago had that been?

"The truth is," David begins, leaning forward, his voice gentle. Like an addiction counselor on one of those reality shows Carolyn used to watch. The ones where a doctor or therapist calmly recounts the havoc someone has created in their life. Chaos is visible to everyone except the subject of the intervention. "You wanted to belong here. You were eager to belong here. And you got your wish." He sits back in the chair, dropping both arms to his sides.

"But I didn't know." She begins but her voice catches in her throat. She saw how Rae was treated. Heard from Gabriella. How badly had she wanted to know anything more?

"Fair enough, but here we are. And you're going to have to trust me."

"Why?" She's lost the defensive edge in her voice.

"Because your survival depends on me."

Maddie laughs. The sound spills from her before she can censor herself. She stares at the lanky young man. The idea of her survival, or anyone's depending on him is silly.

His expression doesn't change.

Maddie covers her mouth with her hand and tries to bring herself back under control. This is just ridiculous. But he seems to believe it. She should humor him.

"Like I said before," David continues, "They've started noticing things. And I can cover for you. But you have to be more discreet. That is, if your choice is what I think it will be."

Maddie shakes her head, confusion showing on her face, "What choice?"

"Sorry, I didn't explain it," David sighs, "You've been here long enough. They are ready to officially accept you. And that means, you have to, um, commit."

Maddie can see beads of sweat forming on the young man's forehead.

"Commit? Like, to a job? Or what?"

"To um," he looks away nervously, rubbing his hands on his legs, "To me. To a um." He still can't look at her, "To marriage."

Under other circumstances, she would have laughed at this as well. But Maddie can see how difficult it was for him to say the words.

"But we've just been on a few dates. I mean we don't really know each other." She begins, but stops short, her mind finally processing David's body language. She feels her face grow red and hot.

He doesn't want to marry me.

She doesn't want to marry him either. Not yet. Maybe not at all. But the realization that he doesn't want to marry her stings.

"But, David, you don't want to do this. Right? I mean you're not asking me to marry you. You're telling me that, what? That my survival depends on marrying you? Which is not really any kind of pickup line let alone a proposal."

David smiles. She's grateful for the break in tension.

"You're right," his eyes meet hers again, "I don't want to marry you. But I can cover for you. If you are willing to cover for me."

"Meaning?"

He begins to answer, then stops, biting his lip in deeper contemplation. He shifts uncomfortably in his chair.

"You know where Rae goes? I mean about the coaching?"

Maddie's eyes widen, she didn't know Rae told others. Or maybe it was just David?

"Yes, she and I have talked. A few times." David answers the question she didn't ask. "I understand. I don't tell their business to other people. But they told me about you. They trust you. So, I feel like I can trust you. But I need to know I can. Because it's coming down to the wire."

"Did you go to coaching?" she asks.

"Once. As a teenager. And it was terrifying enough to convince me that living a lie would be better than going through that again."

A realization forms on the edges of Maddie's awareness. She can't quite articulate it yet, but something is crystallizing in her subconscious. A puzzle close to being solved.

"I'm willing to stay in the closet." David's voice cracks. "I'll get married. Keep up appearances. And do what I can to help people who need it. People like Rae and Gabriella. But if you agree, it won't be a, you know, it won't be the marriage you were expecting."

Maddie sits in silence, trying to make sense of what she's being told.

"I just need you to keep it a secret. And I think you will. I think you understand."

A moment passes as Maddie wrestles with the fog in her mind. Marriage. To a gay man. Who would rather pretend than face the consequences. And what was the alternative for her?

"What is the other option?"

David drops his eyes to examine his shoes. He grips the sides of his seat with both hands. "At best, the other option is that you become a surrogate. A servant in someone's home. An unpaid laborer. But being a surrogate means being, not quite human. Second class. You lose your place in this society."

"And the worst option?"

His silence answers the question.

Images flash in her mind.

The tree. A ladder leaning against it.

Grandma Winnie shouting at Billie Jo "Wait until it's your daughter!"

"Wait," Maddie responds louder than she intended, "what about Rae? Where have they been?"

"When coaching doesn't work," David begins, his face lined with worry, "The next step is prolonged visits to the sanitarium. For etiquette classes."

From the look on his face, Maddie can tell this process has nothing to do with balancing a plate on your head or ballroom dancing.

"And if that doesn't work?"

David closes his eyes.

"They become a sacrifice."

Grandma Winnie's words return to Maddie's mind.

"Wait until it's your daughter"

She blinks, but the man seated across from her fades into a blurry scene. Maddie's vision is clouded. She blinks again harder, hoping to wake up before the thoughts in her mind connect.

But it's not a dream.

Sacrifice.

She pushes the words out with a small voice, trying to ignore the ringing in her ears. Shutting her eyes tight.

"But we can stop it, right? I mean for Rae. There's something we can do to help Rae, isn't there?"

David's stern expression isn't reassuring.

"It's never been done before. But we can try. And it's not just Rae. Gabriella, too. They've been leaving the town. Going to Green-ridge."

"What's wrong with that?" Maddie asks.

"They are bringing food and clothes and things to poor people over the town line. Theoretically, nothing is wrong with it. But it's frowned upon in Silver Spring."

"But Silver Spring makes donations. What's the difference?"
"Well, when Silver Spring does it, the town controls it. They always have. Or at least since it's been Silver Spring. They send a surplus donation once a year at Christmas," David smirks as he says this, "but it's never enough. And it's on purpose."

Maddie nods, recalling the charity groups who used to come through the camps and parking lots giving out baggies of hygiene supplies. The shelters that offered a bed for a fee and with stipulations that most homeless people couldn't abide.

"They both stand out for being…"

He searches his mind for the right word. Maddie garners political correctness isn't a thing up here.

"Different," he settles on the word the way someone may say 'special' when they mean to describe someone who doesn't fit in. "But to break the rules, to undermine the stability of this town? That's a bridge too far. They've been playing with fire."

Maddie recalls the vitriol in the voices of townspeople at the city council meeting. Even the town doctor, speaking of "those people" as if referring to vermin.

An image of rats crawling across the floor at Arianna's wedding flashes through her mind. She has so many questions. But she doesn't want to ask. Part of her doesn't want to know anything more. Wants to retreat to a world of polite small talk and neighborly gestures. Of unlocked doors and wedding plans.

Be careful what you preserve, Grandma Winnie had said.

Was it possible to have all this without the other parts of Silver Spring? Subservience. Racism. Control. If everyone was allowed to be who they are, couldn't Silver Spring still be a place of neighbors and friends and celebration?

Maybe she should stay.

She regards David. He's handsome enough. She always thought so. A marriage to him wouldn't be bad. And as for their platonic secret arrangement? Did it matter?

Maddie hadn't thought about sex much since her life fell apart. Even in her happiest moments at Silver Spring sexual fantasies never crossed her mind. She was distracted instead by other kinds of fantasies. The house. The picket fence. The wedding dress.

Maybe it wouldn't been bad to blend in. And use it to make things better in the long run.

"How can we help them?"

For the first time since her arrival in Silver Spring, Maddie felt self-conscious. She couldn't shake the feeling that people were watching her. In the grocery store. At work. In the library. Sizing her up after her meltdown at the funeral home. Whenever she crossed paths with a couple or family, or a group of friends strolling casually down the street, her admiration for the open and friendly demeanor of the townspeople was replaced by an uneasy suspicion that they were whispering about her once she was out of earshot.

But people handle grief in all different ways, she tried to reason with herself.

Deep inside, she knew better.

People here don't do anything in different ways.

Not if they want to live.

Maddie swallowed the fear. She pushed the revulsion and panic down until it became a lump lodged in the base of her throat. And then a burning in her chest. A hollow ache in the pit of her stomach. She started leaving behind more of her meals, unable to fit the full course in the same stomach busy digesting the truth about the place she'd fallen in love with.

And when she slipped out of sight of the watchful neighbors to meet Gabriella, David, and Rae in different places throughout the town, she couldn't stifle the feeling that she was cheating on someone. Or something. Her clandestine and brief meetings became an act of infidelity she couldn't fully understand.

They met in the small house twice in a row already, so today they agreed to cross paths on a side street near the Main Street shops. Few houses and proximity to conveniences made it an easy spot to appear to randomly meet up, even if their encounter was not truly random at all.

Maddie arrives first. She reaches for her purse instinctively to busy herself with her phone, then remembers she no longer has a cell phone. She hasn't had it for months. She pretends to analyze the window displays of a few shops to pass the time instead.

A model train layout with tiny mountains and models of the Adirondacks- Lake George, Schroon Lake, catches her attention. She follows the landmarks to Lake Placid and even Plattsburgh.

But where was Silver Spring? Or Greenridge for that matter?

"Excuse me, miss, are you a model train enthusiast?" Rae's imitation townie voice startles her.

Maddie catches her breath and releases it in a laugh when she sees Rae's familiar face.

"Sorry, didn't mean to scare you."

"Oh, no, you're okay," Now it's Maddie's turn to be facetious, "it's just that I never expected to run into you here today." She stops short of winking indulgently.

"That's the great thing about Main Street," Rae plays along, "You never know who you'll see. Hey, isn't that David and Gabriella over there?" They point toward an alley and Maddie turns to see the couple emerge, faces serious as they chat quietly.

She recalls with embarrassment the jealousy she once felt seeing them together.

David pretends not to notice them initially, and when he catches Rae's eyes, he waves, the telltale signs of surprise registering on his face.

We're all such good actors, Maddie thinks. *Or at least, we better be.*

"What a nice surprise," Gabriella looks from Rae to Maddie. "I haven't seen you all in so long."

The street is uncharacteristically quiet, but they follow David's lead along the side streets, better to walk than linger. Wouldn't want to be a moving target.

Their conversation continues in a coded version of small talk and innuendo Rae introduced them to a few meetings back.

"I read this book once," Gabriella began, "about these two people who found this time machine that took them back to like the fifties."

"Ugh, that must have been horrible for them," Rae remarked, running their hand along the brick exterior of an ice-cream parlor. The sandwich board sign on the sidewalk, Sweet Family, made Maddie's stomach turn.

"Yeah, it was rough for them, because they really stood out."

"What did they do?" David asked in a tone of light amusement.

"Their time machine broke, of course. So, they were trapped. But then they figured out how to use a car to escape. And They used somebody's car to go back to where they belonged."

"Well, that sounds like it ended well." Maddie smiles.

Rae stops abruptly, causing Maddie to almost run into them. "What if they didn't run away? What if they tried to change the people in the fifties instead?"

David turned, looking into their eyes solemnly.

"That's a good plot twist, for fiction," he said, measuring his words carefully. "But if it had been real life, it would never work."

"Why not?" Rae persists.

"Well for starters," David cracks a smile, "There are no such thing as time machines."

Rae looks down, unable to resist a grin.

"But also," David's face is serious now. Rae meets his eyes again, "They would need a critical mass. One or two people are outnumbered. They would need to return to the fifties with a group if they were serious about overturning the status quo. Otherwise, they would fail."

His words hang in the air. Maddie considers this, her mind turning it over. Pondering. Looking for solutions but coming up short.

Rae's eyes shift toward a storefront window display. Leather shoes lined up in a neat row. "Well luckily, it's a moot point. Because there are no time machines."

They continue walking for a moment before Rae speaks again, "You know, I saw this movie. It was non-fiction." Their voice quivers at the word, fiction.

Maddie glances at the child as they struggle to fight tears. She reaches a hand toward Rae, touching their shoulder.

"What was it about?" she prompts, wondering if she should just let it go.

Rae sighs.

"It was about a place where people carry around guns. There are always fires. Riots. Crime. People are afraid of each other. They lock their doors all the time. Hide everything. They don't even talk to each other."

The group comes to a stop alongside a row of shrubs. No one else in sight, Rae turns to look at Maddie and Gabriella.

"They show the movie. In couching. And at the Sanitarium."

They whisper the word Sanitarium as if it were something to be ashamed of.

"Is it true? That this is what it's like? In the cities?"

"I mean, if you're someone who sits at home watching Fox news all the time it may seem like that," Gabriella folds her arms over her chest. Lips twisted in a look of disgust.

"What's Fox news?" Rae asks, voice timid, as if they aren't sure how to avoid stepping on the landmine that may further upset her.

Gabriella's face softens, "No, I'm not mad at you. They use that same storyline to scare people even outside of Silver Spring. And by the way, that movie you saw? It was fiction. It's not like that. At least, not everywhere all the time."

"I mean, things are different," Maddie begins, "and yeah, in most places people do lock their doors." She recalls how her mother adopted this habit. After her father died and they moved from the suburbs to Poughkeepsie.

"But it's exaggerated. And the message is backwards. They want people to fear people like us," Gabriella gestures to herself and Rae," so you don't pay attention to the people who are the real threat. And they're much fewer and far between than you may think."

Maddie considers this. No one ever actually broke into her house. No one she knew was ever the victim of a random crime. Would it have been the same if they ignored her mother's warnings? If she never locked the door?

A scene flashes in her mind. Walking to school with Carolyn. Passing a group of teens. Their jeans hung low on their hips. Their skin the same shade as her friend's. But something felt different then. Maddie, just entering middle school, had instinctively grabbed her purse, holding it tighter against her side. She didn't even know she made the gesture until she turned to see the look on Carolyn's face.

"Why'd you do that?" Carolyn had asked.

Maddie hadn't answered.

Her friend didn't press her then. They continued their walk to school in silence and by lunchtime it was forgotten.

At least Maddie forgot it. Until now. Her heart sinks. She wonders if Carolyn really did forget. Or if she just stopped bringing it up.

The way Maddie eventually stopped bringing up all her ex, Jeff's bad habits when it became more exhausting to try to change him than it was to just live with all of his annoying behaviors.

In a moment, the timeline of her youth is condensed into glimpses. Laughing at Carolyn in the food court on weekends, sneaking out at night to go to the basketball court, watching the skaters at the park, drifting from one house party to another.

The realization dawns on her, bringing both relief and anger. Relief that she had never been in danger in any of the situations ingrained in her mind from movies, or her mother's subtle insinuations about "bad" neighborhoods. Anger that she had been led to believe she had ever been in danger in the first place. All fading in the blink of an eye into embarrassment that she had been so narrow-minded to fall for it and ultimately, sadness at all she had missed hiding behind the veneer of projected victimhood.

When had she ever truly been in danger in her life?

She recalls then, waking in the early hours, cold and startled. In her car. In a dark corner of a parking lot. Roused from slumber by an older man hovering outside her car window. Well dressed, probably a businessman of some kind, soliciting her for sex.

"You okay?" David asks.

Maddie shakes the memory away.

"Oh, yes. Sorry. Was just thinking about it all."

Rae also looks lost in thought, Maddie realizes. As they continue their walk, the child again breaks the silence.

"So, it's like this everywhere?"

"Like what?" Gabriella asks.

"Like how there's Silver Spring and Greenridge. And the Silver Spring people are always trying to blame everything on the Greenridge people when really, it's the Greenridge people who are in danger?"

Gabrielle nods slowly, turning this over in her mind.

"In a way, yes. Mostly. But substitute the words Silver Spring and Greenridge for 'haves' and 'have nots' or 'powerful' and 'disenfranchised.' It's not always about a geographic barrier. Sometimes it's where you're from. Other times it's your skin color. Religion. Gender. Sexuality. Or beliefs in general."

"Or being poor." Maddie adds.

Gabriella nods. "When all else fails, there's always that."

"They played the movie so much." Rae comments, their voice low.

Maddie is so entrenched in her own thoughts she doesn't initially understand what movie Rae is referring to. Then it hits her. There's a name for it, but Maddie can't recall. When you force someone to face something meant to disturb or scare. Cults do it to indoctrinate people. To disorient them. Make them dependent on the cult leaders. Or to scare them away from leaving by convincing them the rest of the world is dangerous. Maddie wonders which intention was behind the use of this tactic at the Sanitarium.

"I'm sorry. That's messed up. And it's not how people should be treated. Let alone kids." Gabriella puts an arm around Rae and hugs them.

CHAPTER 42

They were careful to head home at different times and take different routes. Gabriella departs first, heading south with David. Rae going North toward home shortly after. Maddie was meant to come home last by heading east, then north, a detour around the small business district and past the park before circling back toward the Harris's home.

Maddie was still deep in thought, their thinly veiled plan and unexpected conversation replaying in her mind when she closed the front door, not expecting anyone else to be in the Harris's living room.

Emily, sitting still and tall on the couch, teacup in hand, gives the appearance of an eerie statue. Her presence registers in Maddie's peripheral vision before Maddie's mind cad assign meaning.

Emily smiles, but her eyes remain still and cold.

Maddie becomes acutely aware of the closed door behind her. A barrier between the world of this afternoon and her walk with David, Gabriella and Rae, and the stifling room into which she entered a moment ago.

She feels as if she's entered a tomb. The grandfather clock in the corner ticks away the seconds.

Maddie forces her mouth into a smile. Or at least, she hopes it looks like a smile. She wonders if her lips are stretched too thin in the shape of a grimace. Like a scared dog.

"Hi, I haven't seen you around." Maddie lets out the words in an awkward rush, immediately wishing she could start over.

Too late.

Emily's perfectly sculpted eyebrows arch slightly. Of course, she's been to the spa, Maddie thinks. Her wedding day is approaching.

"We haven't had time to talk in a long time," Emily maintains a pasted-on appearance of polite welcome. But it doesn't look genuine. There is something plastic and pristine about it. A front for something else.

Maddie starts to head toward the stairs, but Emily continues.

"I was hoping you could join me for some tea."

She eyes the tray on the coffee table. An old-fashioned set with a petite finely decorated teakettle. Another porcelain teacup, the twin to the one in Emily's delicate hand, turned upside down, brim down on a tray. Waiting for its drinker to satisfy its purpose.

Her chance to escape has passed.

Maddie wills her mouth to stretch farther, feels her smile pushing her eyes into a squinting mask.

Something about this feels wrong. But she doesn't know what.

Maddie approaches the sofa, sitting beside Emily. She's careful to retrieve the teacup by the tiny handle, afraid her fingers will be too rough, too heavy, too indelicate to touch such a thing. Maddie nods toward Emily, a gesture that feels more subservient than a salute or even a cheers.

You win.

I'll drink your tea.

A fleeting thought occurs to her. That something may be in it. Some of the medicine left over from what was used to manage Grandma Winnie toward the end of her life. But she can't refuse now.

She pours, careful to stop with as little of the amber liquid as possible in her cup without raising suspicion.

Smoke wafts in a thin stream from her cup, giving her an excuse to set it down on the small matching porcelain dish beside the tray.

"How are you feeling?" Maddie asks, trying to break the silence while keeping Emily's focus off of her. Eager to talk about the bride to be and her prewedding jitters, or the loss of her grandmother, or anything other than what is on Maddie's mind.

"I'm feeling quite well, thank you," her voice more confident, she speaks faster now, "There's just so much to do, planning the wedding and all. And I was so heartbroken over my dear grandmother's death. It's a shame she won't be here to see my special day. But it's like Dan reminded me, she'll be here in spirit."

Emily sips her tea.

Is she bluffing?

Or really that superficial?

"Well, I'm glad you have the wedding to look forward to." Maddie plays along, eyeing her still-steaming cup.

"Oh, there's a lot to look forward to in Silver Spring. What woman wouldn't want a traditional wedding to a good, strong man who will take care of her for the rest of his life?"

Maddie doesn't know how to answer, or even if she is supposed to answer. But Emily doesn't give her a chance. She continues.

"You're really lucky, you know?"

The sudden change in conversation takes Maddie off-guard.

"I am? Why? You're the one getting married to the dream guy, right?" She tries to deflect back to Emily.

"True." Emily sips again, "But you're an outsider."

Emily emphasizes the word 'outsider' as if she is trying to find inspiration in someone's battle with leprosy to make an example.

"You have the chance to live a life everyone like us dreams of. But this is not a chance most people get."

"No," Maddie nods slowly, "I'm sure it isn't."

"In fact," Emily goes on, "We usually discourage visitors. But we recognize our own."

The words fill Maddie with a spark of anxiety. And something else. She can't place it, but a rush of excitement passes down her spine.

"Our own?" Maddie asks, examining Emily's features carefully. Was she suggesting they were long-lost relatives? Distant cousins?

"It's rare that someone is born here who truly isn't fit for this land. It happens. Every so often," Emily avoids eye contact as she says this, and Maddie knows she's talking about Rae. "It's like a runt in a healthy litter. Sometimes these things just happen. But even more unusual is someone from away who belongs here. We can usually spot our own. And we're seldom wrong."

Maddie is still confused. She's heard of Indigenous sayings about people belonging to the land, but she doubts this is what Emily means.

"You make it sound like there's some kind of magic spell. Like Silver Spring gets to pick and choose who comes here and who doesn't."

"Oh, but there is. In a way. People gravitate here when they're meant to be one of us. When they are one of us. They feel a pull. Something like that. Something brings them here."

Emily sips her tea again and this time Maddie forces herself to take a sip from her own cup. It's jasmine and cinnamon and something else she can't place. It burns but she tries to ignore it.

"As long as we keep to our way of life and don't let anyone corrupt our youth or change our ways, we are all just fine. We live in peace. No crime. No worries."

Unless you count murder. Or child abuse.

"Don't you want to live in a nice, quiet place?"

"Sure."

"Silver Spring never has the kinds of problems other places have. You'll never have to worry about not having enough money."

"That's appealing." Maddie isn't lying. She forgot how easy things are in Silver Spring. There's never a shortage of anything important. And her work is easy, but meaningful. And it's enough for her to save up. Her needs are met. She wants for nothing.

"And isn't it nice?" Emily asks.

Maddie drifted momentarily. She doesn't know what she's being asked.

But it is nice. It's nice in Silver Spring.

She smiles, warmth settling into her cheeks. This smile is genuine. Kind. Polite. Because it's nice in Silver Spring.

And it's good to be somewhere nice.

Where people are nice.

And good.

"It's good, isn't it?" Emily asks.

Her eyes are friendly. Warm. They are like jasmine. And cinnamon. And something else.

Maddie giggles. Why was she so worried before?

"Sometimes people wander in who are not so nice," Emily's tone changes.

Maddie sits straighter, alert to the change in the woman's demeanor.

"They try to corrupt our children. Turn them against us. It isn't nice to do that, is it?"

"No, it's not nice."

"It's not nice to interfere with a child's family. To ruin traditions. Is it?"

"No, that's not nice at all."

Another sip.

"I'm so glad you'll be part of my wedding," Emily smiles. The warmth and pleasantness returning to her tone.

"So am I. Weddings are nice."

"Yours will be just as nice." Emily adds.

"My wedding to David."

"Yes, I'm glad you plan on staying."

"Of course. Who wouldn't want to live in Silver Spring?" Maddie asks the question before finishing the last of her tea.

CHAPTER 43

For days, Maddie manages to avoid Emily and Billie Jo except for the obligatory family dinners. Her resolve is clear in the fleeting moments she spends catching up with David or Rae, or Gabriella-although these encounters are becoming rare of late. But within minutes of returning home, Maddie's disgust melts away. Even walking down the hall past Grandma Winnie's old room no longer leaves her with pangs of anger and grief.

When she's home- for the Harris's house is home- it's as if the horrors of Silver Spring are nothing more than a dream. With each day that has passed since tea with Emily, she has adapted more to the idea of marrying David. Living in Silver Spring. Carrying on tradition.

Only the chance sight of Rae or Gabriella reminds her there was something more to her plan. Something only three other people in the town were aware of.

She even forgets the dual existence that nauseates and confuses her in the moments she is reminded of her secret plans. But this memory dissipates as quickly as it arises, and she returns to her days at the Preservation Society and weekends helping Emily with wedding plans and dreaming of her own eventual wedding that will follow.

"A winter wedding is so romantic," Emily commented, squeezing her arm with encouragement as they study seating charts. Plans and diagrams sprawl across the Harris's dining room table. The room is converted to ground zero for wedding planning this weekend before the big day.

"It's like something out of a Hallmark movie," Maddie responds, recalling another point of contention between herself and Carolyn, who couldn't stand the tropes and what had she called them? Patriarchal something-or-other.

"What's a Hallmark movie?" Emily asked, smile unwavering.

Maddie winced, for months she managed to avoid the awkward pop culture explanations, catching herself before referring to shows she used to binge or influencers she used to follow.

"Oh, it's nothing really, it's like, a series of movies made for television and they're dorky and romantic." Maddie hears Carolyn's description escape her lips, realizing her mistake too late.

Emily looks stung by her words.

"Romance isn't dorky. It's what every woman lives for. What makes life worthwhile? Except children."

"Oh, of course," Maddie hurries to soothe her friend, glossing over her own self-contradiction. "It's just that, I mean I used to tell myself it was dorky because…"

Don't do it. Don't talk about your personal life. This could go down a rabbit hole you don't want to follow.

"Because?" Emily prompts her.

Maddie thinks of Jacqui at the convenience store. Her childhood frenemy, graceful as ever, her no-doubt-popular child, who would be Prom Queen someday, in tow. Recalls making small talk awkwardly, hoping Jacqui couldn't tell she just used a restroom sink to bathe herself because she was living in her car.

Because I was homeless with no prospects and no future and surviving by living in parking lots which is really not very romantic, she wants to say.

"I wasn't popular with the guys. Ever," she answers instead. A partial truth. Before being dumped by her best friend, Maddie had a long track record of breakups with various guys who had been willing to give her a chance for a few months or even a year or two before opting out.

Emily furrows her brow, pouting.

God, no, don't do it. Don't pity me.

Emily, in full pity-mode, grabs Maddie into a bear hug and kisses her cheek. It would be sweet if it was just a friendly gesture and not all so saccharine and pathetic.

"It's okay, you're in Silver Spring now, where men know the value of a woman like you. That's why there were so many guys interested in you. But David, he's a real catch."

This news startles Maddie.

"What guys?" she blurts out, catching herself, she backpedals, "I mean, not that I care. Because David, he's a great guy. But just curious, I don't know what you mean?"

"Oh, there were a few men interested in you. But David had it bad for you right away. I could tell. He knew you were different. So, I did you a favor and discouraged the competition."

She winks, her grin both innocent and devilish.

"He thought I was different, huh?" Maddie mumbles.

You have no idea.

He planned it, but not for selfish purposes, which was clear. Was it because he knew she would be the most likely to do… to be open to … something? Something they talked about was on the periphery of her mind but foggy. Were they supposed to start a business together? Or…

Help Rae and Gabriella escape.

Clarity returns like a thunderclap.

"Right," she speaks the word aloud before realizing she's responding to a thought, not something Emily said.

It's no matter, the young woman is back to focusing on her seating plans. She squints, bringing lines to her forehead that weren't there before.

"We really shouldn't seat the Conrads near Betsy Ann Lester."

"They don't like each other?" Maddie doesn't care about small town gossip. She's grateful for the distraction.

"Well, everyone in Silver Spring gets along, so it's not anything bad like what happens in the cities."

She uses the reference Maddie has come to recognize as an allusion to any place that isn't Silver Spring. Outside places are "away" or "the city."

"But there is an issue because Mrs. Conrad has a daughter, Mindy. And Betsy Ann used to have a daughter who was Mindy's close friend. Well, Betsy Ann's daughter got to be of an age when her wickedness was running rampant. She was going astray."

Emily whispers the word "astray" as if she is sharing raunchy details of a sordid affair.

"Did Mindy turn her in?" Maddie guesses, assuming the Conrads would blame their daughter's best friend for doing whatever counts as going astray in Silver Spring.

"Oh, no. That would have solved everyone a lot of heartbreak. But Mindy was influenced by wickedness. At least she started to go down that path, influenced by someone she trusted. Happens every once in a while, thankfully most people learn better and know that when you care about someone, the right thing to do is refer them for coaching."

"What happened?"

"Well, Mindy had a round of coaching and that corrected her er-rored thinking. Fortunately, it wasn't too late. As for her friend, well, she's lost all prospects of a future and has been working as a domestic aid for years now. Her own fault. Still, Betsy Ann is sensitive about it, so it's best to keep them apart from each other. Like over here?"

Emily turns the chart to face Maddie, who only nods nonchalantly, indifferent to who sits where.

Something else is on her mind.

She studies Emily. The young woman's face alternates between giddiness and austerity as she absorbs herself in wedding planning. She's always been kind to Maddie. Treated her like a sister from the start. But Maddie is an outsider.

We recognize our own.

Maddie clears her throat. "What, um, what would happen if Rae-I mean Desirae were to go 'astray'? I mean, what would you do?"

Emily turns to her, her face showing bewilderment. Maddie wonders if she's crossed a line.

"I've already done everything for her that I can. I told our parents at the first sign something was wrong with her." Emily rolls her eyes, frustration showing in her voice, "That child has had so many opportunities. More than most because of who our grandmother was. But she's ruining her chances. I would just as soon she be sent to work as a servant already. She's been an embarrassment to the family."

Maddie tries her best to hold her body still, afraid to reveal her shock. This was not the answer she was expecting.

Emily smiles and hands her a list of names.

"Would you be a dear and help me make sure everyone on the list has been assigned to their place?" she asks, her voice light and pleasant again.

PART THREE

Wedding Plans

CHAPTER 44

Maddie stares at her reflection in the full-length mirror. The bridesmaid's gown is teal. It's not flattering, but she suspects that is the point. All attention should be on the bride, and Emily, she knows, will soak it all up. She's been planning for this day for months. Or for her whole life, Maddie thinks, her eyes catching a glimpse of the doll house in the mirror.

The late July sun is not yet out in full force but already Maddie can tell it will be hot. The morning is hazy. Not the picture-perfect start to the day. Maddie wonders with disappointment how it is possible that the weather would not cooperate with such a special occasion.

Because it isn't Camelot, the Carolyn in her mind reminds her. Maddie's cheeks flush. Had she really bought into the idea that the land and the town could magically summon the people it sought and command the weather?

She looks in the mirror one last time. Her hair, free to grow now that she has the benefit of indoor plumbing and a paycheck with which she can afford trips to the hairdresser, hovers just above her shoulders. Yet like the weather, it refuses to cooperate. Rather than conforming to her guidance, no amount of brushing will keep the wavy brown curls from expanding with the humidity and finding their way into tangles. She runs her fingers through her tresses again before surrendering.

Emily's wedding is Silver Spring's equivalent of a celebrity event, Maddie learns. Instead of a limo, the wedding party is picked up by a series of horse-drawn carriages.

"It's a tradition," Billie Jo explains.

The matriarch is radiant. Maddie has observed her evolution to self-assuredness since the death of her mother. She never seemed to grieve in any way Maddie could recognize. Today, she and Mark beam with pride as they file in to a carriage will share with Emily and Rae. Rae walks slowly as if their pace is the only act of resistance available. Rae wears the same teal dress as the rest of the bridesmaids. They pull at the skirt periodically, as if trying to stretch it into a more comfortable fit or remove something offensive from their skin to no avail.

Maddie is the last one in the carriage. She sits beside Rae and gives the child's arm a reassuring squeeze when their parents aren't watching. Rae looks up at her and smiles. It's more of a smirk.

Dan and the groomsmen take a separate carriage.

"Can't see the bride before the wedding. It's bad luck!" Emily reminds her as the horses take off.

Maddie smiles, but the reference reminds her of the last wedding they attended. She breaks into a cold sweat. The horses' gallop keeping time with a song. She hears a piano playing. It could be her father, or Grandma Winnie.

Or Emily, seated at the altar, hands flying over the keys as music echoes through the church. Maddie surveys rows of heads, necks and shoulders cropping up from the backs of pews. Light shines through a stained-glass window and plays on the amber and yellow beads of a hatpin in front of her.

It shimmers, gold and yellow.

Like a sunflower.

Maddie's heart picks up pace.

Far from the sound of hooves or the jostling of the carriage, Maddie is haunted by each note. She can't relax. Eyes shifting to her left and then her right, she's lost in a sea of anonymous faces, all eyes on the altar where Emily sits upright and focused on the piano. The altar, where Arianna should have been already.

But never will be.

The song drops into a minor key. Emily slams her fingers onto the piano. Choppy. Disjointed, no longer music but a temper tantrum of keys attached to hammers hitting strings. Suffocating out a melody.

Maddie looks for someone to react. But everyone else sits frozen, their faces blank. Even when the screaming begins.

Maddie turns to see the groom.

"She's gone!" he screams, collapsing to the floor in the back of the church.

A hand closes over Maddie's knee, she jolts in her seat, turning again to the front of the church where Emily now hovers over her.

"You're next."

Maddie gasps.

Laughter erupts around her, bringing her back to the present.

She blinks as the realization sets in. She was daydreaming. Or remembering. Or panicking. Or some combination of the three.

"What?" What do you mean?" she asks.

Emily, seated across from her, leaning uncomfortably close and spilling over with tulle and lace, grins ear to ear.

"You're next. Your wedding will be next. Aren't you excited?" She doesn't have a chance to answer.

"What do you think she was daydreaming about? Her special day with David, of course!" Billie Jo chimes in.

"Of course," Maddie responds too quickly, trying to sound convincing.

The carriage pulls up to the back entrance of the church and the wedding party is ushered into a side room. Its mossy carpeting is worn and dated. Bookshelves line one wall and a few chairs are set in a circle. Maddie thinks it may be where they hold AA meetings, but then remembers where she is.

I doubt Silver Spring has AA.

Emily squeals, a high-pitched and adolescent noise, as several bridesmaids file into the room. They hug each other and Maddie steps aside to give them space. She spots Rae on the far side of the room, studying the spines of dusty old tomes on the bookshelf. They look out of place even with the same teal dress as everyone else.

Maddie wonders if she also looks out of place. She can smile and nod along with the small talk, but she's not feeling the wedding festivities.

She tries to force the happiness she's expected to feel. For Emily's sake.

And for the town.

The thought occurs to her from out of nowhere.

After so much loss. The town needs this.

The organ music begins, their cue to line up and start the procession. The chatter and laughter fades to nervous whispers and giggling. Maddie steps toward the line, behind Emily's lifelong friends but before Rae and then the bride herself. The music continues and Maddie feels tears well in her eyes. The anxiety she felt in the carriage moments ago has dissipated. She passes the display of flowers, and follows the lead of the other bridesmaids, retrieving a bundle of lavender and eucalyptus tied with ribbon around a collection of lilies.

She doesn't see the shadow dart along the floorboards.

Maddie wipes a tear from the corner of her eye, smooths her hair into place, and follows the procession, oblivious to the rats watching from underneath the table.

CHAPTER 45

Earlier that day, as she stood in a line of bridesmaids at the altar, Maddie looked out at the rows of admiring faces. She recognized most of the townspeople because it's Silver Spring. Her home. She'd beamed, feeling right at home in the chapel, wearing her teal bridesmaid's gown, her hair perfectly set in place.

Hadn't someone once said teal was her color?

Standing on the dance floor, watching Emily and Mark begin their first dance as husband and wife, she looks down at her flowing satin skirt. So flattering. Someone touches her shoulder lightly. Maddie turns to see David, looking handsome in his suit, matching the rest of the groomsmen. She's surrounded by the wedding party, all matching pairs, perfectly arranged like the sugar-sprinkled flowers that climb the tiers of the wedding cake.

An hour ago, as they stood at the altar, Maddie lost herself in fantasy. She imagined herself in Emily's place. Imagined the lilies and delphiniums were for her. She even caught herself looking down at her hand, expecting to see a glistening row of diamonds on her ring finger.

She hadn't pictured David with her.

Now, as she takes his hand and joins him in a dance, gliding past the bride and groom. She stares into his eyes. They sway with the rhythm of some generic wedding song Maddie's heard before but never really paid attention to. The remaining guests join in the dance, two by two, swaying to the music in the low lighting.

With the lights low, he looks like someone else. Everyone looks different in the shadows, she thinks. And it can be like that. Keep the lights low and she doesn't have to be Madison, who sleeps in her car and wanders from one lot to another when the sun sets. She can be Maddie. And she doesn't need David, she realizes.

She just needs Silver Spring.

Her eyes wander around the reception hall, tracking the couples who pass them on the dance floor. Surely, there could be other options. Hadn't Emily said there were others who were interested in her?

"And now," A voice she recognizes as Billie Jo calls everyone to attention. She looks radiant, proud, and regal. Billie Jo stands with a glass raised, "A toast, to my beautiful daughter, Emily."

Applause spreads through the room

Emily blushes. A beautiful, blushing bride. Not a bossy wife. Maddie smiles. This can be her life.

David squeezes her arm. She meets his eyes and sees the discomfort in his expression.

She smiles, reassuringly.

He can't find out.

CHAPTER 46

Maddie couldn't remember the last time she felt as giddy as she did by the time she returned home from Emily's wedding. She replayed the events of the day in her mind. Dancing with David, catching up with her friends. She'd spotted Gabrielle and Rae at some point, looking sour as ever.

Sitting on the edge of the unicorn bed, staring at the dollhouse, Maddie vaguely recalled some discussions she'd had with those two. Something about the town, its history, and some awful, no, regrettable elements of its past.

But wasn't that everywhere?

And you can't judge people from the past by today's standards, she reminds herself.

That was a different time. Things are different now.

What about what Gabriella told you? A renegade voice in the depths of her mind asked.

She misunderstood. Maddie spoke the words aloud to the empty room, confident in herself. Maddie was sure of it now. She grew up in a diverse neighborhood. She was sensitive to things like that, and she hadn't seen any racism in Silver Spring.

The dollhouse fades from sight, replaced by an image in her mind. A photo of Grandma Winnie surrounded by townspeople, standing before a tree. Someone left the ladder in place.

Maddie shivers.

No recent racism, she corrects herself.

She must have been overreacting. Caught up in some kind of hysteria. It wasn't that bad, she reminds herself. Not bad enough to warrant leaving.

She stands now, facing the dollhouse, running a finger along the dusty imitation living room. Her wedding wouldn't be like Emily's. She would have no father to walk her down the aisle. Sadness spikes at her heart. She shuts her eyes tight, then opens them again. Her gaze shifts to the tiny wooden dining room table, surrounded by miniature chairs. She moves them around, picturing a family gathering for a meal.

It wouldn't be that bad. And if it is, she can change it. She could make it better.

Maddie turned toward the closet, where her teal gown hung. A memento of her day and the promise of a future in Silver Spring.

You're next, Emily had said.

Smiling, Maddie crawled into the bed, settling under the comfort of warm blankets. Her feet ached from dancing all day and it took little time for her to drift to sleep.

*　*　*

In her dream, Maddie is in the apartment she shared with Carolyn.

And where was Carolyn? Maddie wonders, smoothing the layered tulle skirt of her wedding gown. She raises her head, facing the full-length mirror. Her hair has grown out fully, down past her shoulders. It isn't frizzy today, but wavy and silky.

The top of her gown is outlined in pearls. The elegant look she wanted. And Carolyn promised to help with her veil. Where was she?

Maddie wanders from the bedroom to the living room down a short hallway. Carolyn is there. She's not dressed for the wedding. Instead, sweats and a t-shirt that look more appropriate for cleaning or…

Moving.

Carolyn is packing boxes. She breathes loudly and Maddie wants to yell. Wants to tell her she's being too dramatic and why isn't she dressed for the wedding but before she can speak a word, she hears her own voice coming from across the room.

She's frozen now. An apparition watching the scene play out. Neither Carolyn nor her past self- she assumes that's who it is- can see her.

Her past self crosses her arms, offering an apology that, if she's honest now, sounds like an accusation.

"You just don't get it," Carolyn responds, and Maddie can see now she wasn't just breathing hard from packing. Carolyn is crying. "You think this is a game because it doesn't matter to you."

"That's not true," Maddie yells, at the same time her past self echoes her words.

Carolyn turns away, "You always do this. You're supposed to have my back, but when something goes wrong, I'm just the 'angry Black woman' and you get to be the good guy. You threw me under the bus with the landlord and now my ass is on the line!"

"I'll explain-"

"No," Carolyn turns to face her past self, "You've already explained enough. We were supposed to be in this together, but when push comes to shove you did what was right for you. Like you always do."

She hears her past self argue. Say it isn't true. But now she knows better. Her heart sinks. Tears well in her eyes as she relives the moments she let down her best friend for the last time.

Her younger self storms out the door leaving Carolyn.

"You were right," she offers to the apparition who can't hear her.

"It backfired anyway." Maddie smirks, "I ended up living in my car for months. So, I guess you can say I learned my lesson."

Had she?

Carolyn resumes packing. Maddie follows her around the room, trying to catch her eyes. Wanting to get her attention. She's no longer wearing a wedding gown but jeans and a sweatshirt. Just like the last day she saw the woman who was like a sister to her growing up.

Carolyn had moved to another apartment with her cousin, Amanda. A woman Maddie never felt accepted by. She remembered Amanda once telling Carolyn not to trust white women when she didn't think Maddie was in earshot.

She hears the door open again and turns to see Emily.

"Are you ready?" Emily smiles at her.

Maddie looks back at her friend, but Carolyn is gone. She returns to answer Emily, but now she, too, has disappeared. In her place, the figure she recognizes. The woman who has been haunting her since she first came to Silver Spring. She smiles, arms and legs moving in quick jerky motions like a sped-up horror movie.

The figure lunges toward Maddie who wakes in a cold sweat.

CHAPTER 47

Maddie's stomach is sick. In the past twenty-four hours her reality has ricocheted from euphoria back to confusion and dread. The thought of staying in Silver Spring now made her nauseas. She stuffed the teal dress in the back of the closet, unable to look at it. Mind whirling as she tried to recall what made her so enraptured with the idea of settling down here now that she knows….

Knows…

Something. It seems distant now. But something about the past. About her past. Or the town's past. Was there a difference? Was it just a dream?

She looked for Gabriella that afternoon but couldn't find her. Thinking back, she hadn't really had a chance to talk to her, or Rae, or even David aside from small talk at the wedding. Had it really been weeks since she'd seen them?

A magenta sun set that evening as Maddie returned home from her last-ditch effort to check the park, the guesthouse, and the library for her friends. She came up short at each location and didn't want to ask around. No need to drum up attention.

Back at the Harris's, Emily was home. There was no sign of anyone else when Maddie walked in. She thought it strange that Emily would be here so soon after her wedding. But then, she never heard the young woman speak of a honeymoon.

Because no one ever leaves.

"I've been meaning to talk to you," Emily greeted her with a smile. Maddie's eyes arched in surprise.

"Oh?" She slumped into the rocking chair by an end table. The one Grandma Winnie had napped in many nights. Maddie pushes the image of the older woman from her mind before she could go too far and recall the last time she saw her alive.

Or dead.

Emily, holding a steaming teacup atop a matching saucer, sits on the couch, resting the cup and saucer on the coffee table. Her eyes are icy blue, smile unchanging.

"About the other day."

Maddie doesn't know which day she is referring to but doesn't interrupt.

"I can tell you've been thinking about things. Considering what we talked about. About you and David and your future here."

Maddie blushes, trying to hide her discomfort. Emily pauses to sip her tea.

"I have been thinking about some things," Maddie hints, "I was actually feeling really optimistic, was going to ask what you put in my tea." She studies Emily's eyes to see if she registers a knowing look. Or will she take Maddie's words as a lighthearted joke.

Emily remains poised, but her gaze is probing. Maddie shivers.

Emily raises her eyebrows slightly, "I have no need to put anything in anyone's tea. Except a little sugar sometimes. Silver Spring is entrancing enough. When people come here, this place has a hold on them." Her voice turns serious, "Any thoughts or desires you have, they are all your own." She sips again and now Maddie thinks she is the one being studied.

A chill traces her spine. Maddie shifts in her seat, she feels like she's squirming under the young woman's gaze.

"Anything you think you want, it's all you, Maddie. Silver Spring just helps you to be," she pauses, breathing deeply as if inhaling flowers, "honest with yourself."

Maddie's ears ring. She tries to catch her breath as the room spins. Emily must have seen the change in her face, because the next thing Maddie knows, the young woman is standing in front of her, placing a teacup in her hand. Jasmine. Maddie drinks. And as she does, she knows it's true. Somehow, she knows. This is her home.

CHAPTER 48

It took three more days for Maddie to be sure. But on that Thursday afternoon, she found Billie Jo reading a paperback in the living room. Her legs curled behind her. Maddie thinks she looks like a teenager, relaxed, and lost in fantasy.

Maddie wonders if she should let the woman be and return later, but before she can backtrack, Billie Jo looks up and smiles, catching her eyes.

"Hello, dear. I haven't seen much of you since the wedding. Is everything okay?"

"Yes, I've just been busy."

Billie Jo puts her book down, bent spine facing up forming a tent. She leans forward on the couch, rubbing her hands together excitedly, "Of course, you'll be the next one married, are you and David making plans?"

We were, Maddie thinks, not catching the double meaning in her own thoughts right away.

"Um, actually," she steels herself, "that's what I wanted to talk to you about."

Billie Jo pats the cushion beside her, and Maddie sits on the couch. She realizes how much Billie Jo has become like a mother to her. More than a mother, her own mother was barely home. She could never trust her mother to have a conversation like this.

"I found some things out. About David."

At first, she was only going to tell the woman about David. Let the town deal with him, she could find her other options that way.

But as the conversation went on, Maddie feels so comfortable with Billie Jo, she goes further than she intended.

"And there's something about Desirae too."

"Yes?" Billie Jo looked nonchalant when Maddie told her about David's sexuality. The secrets he confided in her. Maybe Billie Jo wouldn't even care, she told herself. But now the woman looks concerned.

"I, um, I've been meeting with her. And Gabrielle," she begins, then adds quickly, "Just to keep an eye on her, she's so young and impressionable. But I'm concerned."

Billie Jo leans back, her eyes wide, cheeks turning red. "Go on."

"Well, I know she's had some problems. And it's not your fault. You're a perfect mother. She's had every chance here really. I think she's been having some bad influences. And she's going to try to run away. With Gabrielle. Soon."

Maddie knows this because the night before last she gathered with Gabriella and Rae to go over plans. They were supposed to leave tonight. All of them. And David. They planned to sneak out, take her car, and head for Greenridge. There, a friend Rae met sneaking out to bring food to the homeless would help them get farther away, even leave the state if need be. They talked about Vermont. But Maddie didn't tell all of the plan. She left the details out. And of course, her intention to go with them before she changed her mind.

Billie Jo's face looks somber. Her mouth turned down in an arc of disapproval. She breathes a heavy sigh and nods slowly.

"I'm glad you told me this. I'll take care of it now, before things get out of hand." Billie Jo pats Maddie's knee, rising from the couch, she heads for the stairs.

Maddie follows her, feeling relieved but also anxious. She repeats the reasons in her mind, convincing herself she did the right thing as they ascend the stairs. Billie Jo heads for Rae's room and Maddie almost crashes into her when she stops short in the doorway.

The room is empty. Rae's window is open. Just like it was when Maddie discovered the child was sneaking out at night. She sucks in her breath as if punched in the stomach.

Billie Jo almost pushes her out of the way, rushing past her. The woman flies down the stairs, stomping in her haste. She's out the door before Maddie can even make it back to the landing. By the time Maddie follows her out the front door and to the driveway, Billie Jo has already hoisted the garage door open, the old-fashioned way.

Tools are arranged neatly on a workbench. A row of rakes and brooms hang from hooks along the walls. But in place of Maddie's car, an empty space.

How long have they been gone?

Maddie hadn't noticed. She hasn't driven her car since she's been here and had no reason to check on it. It must have been yesterday. Or early this morning. They couldn't have gotten far.

CHAPTER 49

Gabriella

Gabriella paces in the alley, biting her nails. Her footsteps echo in the dark and she shudders with an unrelenting fear that someone can hear her. Even when she stands still, her heart beats too loud. She checks her watch again. Twelve forty-five. They're both late.

In the stillness, she hears a distant shuffling and looks to her right. A silhouette hurries down the alley. Short, features invisible under baggy clothes. Rae. Gabriella releases the breath she's been holding.

Moments later, David arrives too.

"We don't have long," Gabriella begins. "I asked you both to meet me here because something is wrong with Maddie."

"What do you mean?" David asks, his face growing pale.

"She's been quiet. She's not as… present. Did you notice last night at our meeting? She hardly said a word."

"Maybe she's just tired?" Rae offers.

"No, I've seen this before. She's getting cold feet."

"Do you think she's told anyone?" David asks.

"No, I don't think it would be a secret for long if she did," Rae answers quickly. "So, what should we do? Confront her?"

"No time. We have to go. Sooner than planned. Before she has the chance to intervene." Gabriella is breathing fast now. She looks from Rae's eyes to David's and can tell they understand. It's now an emergency. They can't take the time they wanted to pack and prepare.

"I'll get the car tomorrow when everyone's gone to work," Rae offers.

"Can you drive?" David asks, his eyes quizzical.

"Mostly."

"Okay, that's not ideal but then nothing about this is. Grab only the most important things you need. David, you and I should head toward Greenridge. Meet at the town line."

"We should leave at night, it's safer." David suggests.

"But taking the car at night isn't." Rae adds, "Unless I grab the car in the daytime, bring it to Greenridge, and then meet you both there tomorrow night?"

"Okay, let's hope this works."

"It has to." David adds, his voice trembling.

PART FOUR

Fall Bride

CHAPTER 50

Autumnal Equinox

It's warm for late September. A perfect day for a wedding, Maddie thinks. Her gown isn't white tulle and satin. There are no pearls lining the top. Her hands are warm, and sweat soaks into the leaves and stems of her bouquet. The lilacs and daffodils weren't her choice.
Tradition.

She smiles, hoping no one can tell how little sleep she got last night. Townspeople gather around her on this adults-only occasion. She recognizes the owner of the pizzeria, and Francine the Librarian. And there's Frank DePew, who took Grandma Winnie's place as the oldest person in Silver Spring and the last of the founding members.

She glances down at the apricot dress, skirt hovering just above the sun-burnt grass. Someone said it was her color and she agrees. So flattering. The gown is simple for a wedding dress. Her forehead itches and she reaches a hand to adjust the crown of leaves and pinecones, acorns, and tiny white flowers whose name she's already forgotten. She followed their instructions and made the crown herself, as was custom for Silver Pride.

For a moment, her mind drifts to a cold morning in another lifetime. Leaving a restroom, her hair cropped short. Running unexpectedly into Jacqueline.
If only she could see me now.

She shakes the strange thought away. Today is her big day. Silver Pride. The festival they'd all been waiting for. A celebration of the harvest. A flash blinds her, and she blinks rapidly before the park is restored to its usual shades of green. Mr. Winnock smiles, waving a hand from behind his camera. Maddie waves in return.

"Are you ready to take your vows?" Billie Jo asks, approaching her in purposeful strides. She is austere for this occasion. No beaming smile like the day of Emily's wedding.

Is she?

Maddie doesn't know. But there is only one acceptable answer. She's gone too far. She nods quickly, before she can change her mind. In the distance, Emily regards her solemnly, standing beside her husband. For a moment, Maddie looks for Rae out of habit before her memory corrects her.

Rae is gone. Along with Gabriella, and even David.

The one that got away. She almost laughs.

Billie Jo holds out her arm and Maddie lets the older woman guide her down the aisle amidst the trees. Amber and crimson leaves line the path, but the trees haven't finished shedding. Their shade an occasional reprieve from the afternoon sun.

Billie Jo walks slowly, gracefully down the path toward a towering oak. Townspeople don't sit for this ceremony. They stand on either side of the path, watching her. She tries to ignore their eyes but wonders how they are judging her. Weak? Compliant? Dangerous?

Do they still see her as one of them?

She catches the eye of Dr. Needham, her mind flashes to the evening of the town meeting. She recalls his outraged tone as he railed against the homeless of Greenridge, only to be so attentive when she passed out. What did he think of her now?

Almost at the end of the path, the oak where an altar should be. The town council stands watching her. They will officiate, Billie Jo explained.

A week after her friends escaped, the woman sat her down in the living room and offered her a cup of tea. "We don't go searching for people," she said. Her voice was curt. Maddie thought at the time that she would show more emotion if it had been a lost cat or dog let alone her child. "The town has a way of picking and choosing who belongs here. They made their own choices. So be it."

Billie Jo sipped her tea and Maddie mirrored her, although the beverage was still too hot for her comfort. When Billie Jo didn't continue, Maddie broke the silence, "So, now that David is gone, I guess I should begin looking for someone new?"

She hadn't expected Billie Jo to laugh.

"I mean, not to sound presumptuous, but Emily mentioned other men were interested…" her voice trails off as she watches something pass over Billie Jo's face.

The woman set her teacup on the saucer, and Maddie thought she could see Emily at her mother's age in the future, their gestures were identical.

"Dear," Billie Jo began, but her voice wasn't nurturing this time, "I'm afraid that is no longer an option."

Maddie sucked in her breath, her hands turned cold, and she almost dropped her teacup, but managed to regain control.

She blinks back tears now, not wanting to summon the desperate feeling of each wall closing in. Steadying her breath, she looks around at the watchful faces. The canopy of fall leaves fanning her from above. There are no walls to close in here.

"It will be like a wedding, of sorts," Billie Jo's voice plays in her mind.

She focuses on the town Council, five men whose names she can't recall stand in the place of a priest.

"You'll be married to the town." Billie Jo had explained that afternoon in the living room over tea.

"At Silver Pride. A fall bride, devoted to serving Silver Spring." The woman smiled, her eyes piercing, as she raised the teacup to her mouth.

She now stands before the council. Each dressed in maroon robes.

It's better than the alternative.

She thinks of Gabriella. And David. They called it a Surrogate. They didn't mention the ceremony in which Surrogates, the

Fall Brides, were celebrated for one day, and then condemned to a life of loneliness and toil.

Maddie bites her bottom lip. For a moment, she recalls Jacqueline, her childhood frenemy. Maddie remembers seeing her unexpectedly at the convenience stop along the highway before she ended up in Silver Spring. Jacqueline, with her daughter at her side, living the dream.

And I am, too.

An older man from the town council with a greying beard and bear-looking jowls steps forward from the group. He raises his right hand, and Maddie shifts her bouquet to mirror this gesture.

"Repeat after me," he begins.

She complies. Reciting the vows that will spare her from death in this year's harvest. Had anyone opted to take her place, they could have offered as she walked down the aisle. But the town had been silent.

Married to the town, she repeated in her mind. *Not so bad.*

"To uphold our way of life…" he says, and she repeats.

"To uphold our values…"

She repeats him line by line and is surprised to feel comfort. Emily was right. She wanted this all along. Her own thoughts. Her own desires. She was married to the town.

And I will be a good wife, she thinks.

CHAPTER 51

By the time they reached Saratoga Springs, Gabriella had to stop for gas. This time, she didn't feel as panicked. They were far from Silver Spring here. She took her time inside the gas station and was surprised when she returned to the car. David anwere both ducking low, in the back seat.

"Can we just keep going for a while?" David asks when Gabriella closed the door and pulled her seatbelt into place.

"Sure, why what's wrong?"

"This place. It's creepy. It reminds me too much of home- of Silver Spring."

Gabriella nodded, understanding.

"Next time we stop we'll be in another state. I don't think you have anything to worry about." Gabriella reassures them.

"Until next time," Rae adds casually.

Gabriella eyes her in the rearview mirror.

"What do you mean, next time?"

"We have to go back. For the people in the encampment at Greenridge."

"It's too risky," David argues.

"He's right," Gabriella adds.

"But you know what will happen to them," Rae pushes back.

Gabriella thinks they are talking to David. She doesn't know what will happen. Right now, she doesn't want to know. They drive on in silence for almost an hour before Rae speaks up again.

"How did you know Maddie was going to turn us in?"

Gabriella pauses, considering how to answer, and decides to be honest, "I never trust white women."

Diogenes Kaufman (they/them) is an author, LCSW, and occasional gonzo journalist whose novels published by Trash Panda Press include *Frank from Jersey* (2024).

Work under previous name, Angela Kaufman, includes Siskiyou Prize in Environmental Literal Finalist *Quiet Man* (2020), *Golden Apple* (2021), *Murder in the Gilded City* (2022). Nonfiction books include *Queen Up! Reclaim Your Crown When Life Knocks You Down-Unleash the Power of Your Inner Queen* (Conari, 2018).